Murder
in the
Manger

Debbie Young

Copyright Information

MURDER IN THE MANGER
by Debbie Young

© Debbie Young 2017
Published by Hawkesbury Press 2017
Hawkesbury Upton, Gloucestershire, England
Cover design by Rachel Lawston of Lawston Design

ISBN 9781911223214 (ebook)
ISBN 978-1-911223-22-1 (paperback)

About the Author

Debbie Young writes warm, witty, feel-good fiction.

Her Sophie Sayers Village Mystery series of seven stories runs the course of a year in the fictional Cotswold village of Wendlebury Barrow.

Her humorous short stories are available in themed collections, such as *Marry in Haste*, *Quick Change* and *Stocking Fillers*, and in many anthologies.

She is a frequent speaker at literature festivals and writers' events, and is founder and director of the free Hawkesbury Upton Literature Festival.

A regular contributor to two local community magazines, the award-winning *Tetbury Advertiser* and the *Hawkesbury Parish News*, she has published two collections of her columns, *Young by Name* and *All Part of the Charm*, which offer insight into her own life in a small Cotswold village where she lives with her Scottish husband and their teenage daughter.

*For the latest information about Debbie's
books and events, visit her Writing Life website,
where you may also like to join her free Readers' Club:*
www.authordebbieyoung.com

Also by Debbie Young

Sophie Sayers Village Mysteries
Best Murder in Show
Trick or Murder?
Murder by the Book (coming spring 2018)

Short Story Collections
Marry in Haste
Quick Change
Stocking Fillers

Single Short Story Ebooks
Lighting Up Time
The Owl and the Turkey
The War of the Peek Freans Light Wounded

Essay Collections
All Part of the Charm:
   A Modern Memoir of English Village Life
Young By Name:
   Whimsical Columns from the Tetbury Advertiser

To Lucienne Boyce,
for her wit, wisdom and kindness

"God bless us, every one."
Charles Dickens

"Never go to meet trouble half way."
Joshua Hampton

1 Away in a Manger

It was when the stable animals developed the power of speech that I realised the cast were departing from my nativity play script.

"Do you think your baby Jesus would like a cuddle, Mrs Virgin?" asked a small sheep politely.

"Hoi, first go for shepherds!" said an older boy with a tea-towel on his head, elbowing the sheep aside.

The small sheep scowled. "I asked first."

A larger sheep pointed accusingly at Mary. "She's the virgin around here. I think she should make you take turns nicely."

The small sheep and the shepherd made a dash across the stable floor, both arriving at the manger at the same time and grabbing the Baby Jesus. The plastic doll fell in pieces to the flagstone floor, leaving the shepherd holding its left leg and the sheep its head. The congregation gasped in horror.

The larger sheep put his hands on his hips. "Now look what you've done. You've broken Baby Jesus."

As he spoke, a chilling wail rang out from the back pew and ricocheted down the aisle to the front of the church. All eyes turned to stare at its source, sheep and shepherd forgotten.

"My baby! You've murdered my baby!"

A shadowy figure leapt from the back pew and legged it up the aisle to the nave, her shawl falling back to reveal a jumble of fair curls streaming out behind her.

Pushing the children out of her way, she kicked the broken doll aside and burrowed her hands down into the manger, as if looking for buried treasure.

"This isn't the Lucky Dip, you know," said the larger sheep crossly.

Finding nothing but hay, she seized the manger in both hands and tipped it upside down, perhaps expecting to find something valuable tucked away down a crack in the wood. Drawing herself up to her full height, she then turned to Mary.

"He was there an hour ago. I put him there myself."

Mary stared, speechless.

The woman turned to face the congregation, polling the room with an accusing finger. "All right, this is a church, isn't it? So confess! Which of you has stolen my baby?"

2 The Interloper

I should have known that allowing my ex-boyfriend Damian to get involved in my play would lead to disaster. Not that he gave me much choice, turning up on my doorstep like a stray cat.

On the first Sunday morning in November, after a hearty breakfast, I left Hector's flat above his bookshop and strolled light-footed down the High Street towards my cottage. In front gardens along the way, evergreen leaves shone with dew, and spiders' webs twinkled in the morning light.

I was looking forward to spending a quiet day on my own at home, basking in the memories of the night before. Hector planned to spend Sunday visiting his parents at their retirement bungalow on the Somerset coast. I made my excuses not to join him. Meeting his parents this early in our relationship would have been far too soon. Plus he didn't actually invite me.

Like the stout marmalade cat blinking companionably at me from a drystone wall, I had fallen on my feet when I moved to the Cotswold village of Wendlebury Barrow. I'd found kind neighbours, good friends and an agreeable local job in which my handsome and charismatic boss, now my boyfriend, nurtured my ambition to write books.

My Great Auntie May used to say we make our own luck in this world, but by leaving me her cottage in her will, she'd given me a head start for mine.

As I spotted the November parish magazine in the window of the village shop, I remembered the December issue's deadline for my "Travels with my Aunt's Garden" column. I was planning something Christmassy about her trio of fir trees.

The December issue would also advertise the nativity play I was writing for the Wendlebury Players and the village primary school children to perform together, along with a live donkey. A good audience was guaranteed for my debut as a playwright. What could possibly go wrong?

My post-Hector smile turned to a puzzled frown as I reached the brow of the hill and my cottage came into view. Outside stood a white van. Just like Damian's, I thought. Just like the one he had converted into a camper van for his travelling English language theatre company. The sight still brought back bitter memories. I'd been subsidising the costs of Damian's van for four years before we parted.

Surely this couldn't be Damian's van. It was probably a tradesman's. My elderly next-door neighbour Joshua must be having a domestic emergency. If so, he'd done well to get someone to come out to attend to it first thing on a Sunday morning.

What a coincidence, I thought, drawing closer. The back door was covered with European flag stickers, as was Damian's. Maybe it was a Polish plumber. Or one who used his van for his European holidays.

Unlikely, however, that his business might also be called Damian Drammaticas, which was emblazoned down the van's side. Nerves jangling, I broke into a run.

4

As I crossed the road to my front gate, the van's nearside door slid open, and a dishevelled figure with shaggy blond hair jumped down on to the kerb.

"Where the hell have you been?"

Damian clearly hadn't been to charm school since I'd left him.

A number of combative responses sprang to mind: "None of your business", "What's it to do with you?" and "In bed with my new boyfriend who brought me breakfast on a tray, which you never did once in seven years together."

But his aggression couldn't diminish my post-Hector glow.

"Hello, Damian," I said calmly, though my heart was racing, and not in the way it did when I spotted Hector on arrival at work. "What brings you here?"

If he'd come to tell me he loved me after all, he was too late. The vacancy for boyfriend had been filled, though, truth to tell, Hector and I were still at the probation stage, with the option of notice on either side should the position not suit.

Damian's answer caught me out. "Work."

"You told me when I left you that there'd be zero employment in a little village like Wendlebury Barrow."

That was one of many reasons he'd dreamed up for me to stay with him. He'd also wanted me to sell the cottage and buy him a new van with the proceeds.

"Ah, but I've found the perfect vacancy. Director of the local theatre group."

"You mean you're bringing Damian Drammaticas to Wendlebury?" I glanced at the van, fearing the rest of his dreadful company might be about to spring out.

"No, just me. Damian Drammaticas is resting. We've no more bookings till spring."

5

"But the nearest theatres are miles away. Where will you be working – Bristol? Bath? Cheltenham?"

He permitted himself a satisfied smile.

"No, guess again."

I looked once more at the van, wondering whether a new girlfriend might be lurking in the back, listening in.

"But you're definitely on your own?" A new girlfriend would have been fine by me.

"Yep."

I shivered, my previous glow now dispersing like the morning mist.

"Then I suppose you'd better come in and tell me your plans."

I fumbled in my pocket for my door key.

He grinned, and patted my shoulder patronisingly. "I thought you'd never ask."

3 New Directions

As I turned to close the front door behind us, Hector sailed past in his Land Rover, head turned as if hoping to spot me. When he saw Damian's van, he almost crashed into it. Too late for him to see, I blew him a wistful kiss.

I led Damian through to the kitchen.

"So tell me the truth now." I took the kettle to the sink and turned on the tap to fill it. "Have you really got a local job, or are you on the run from something?"

He pulled out a chair and sat down at the kitchen table. "What, you mean like a murder or a bank robbery?"

As I slammed the kettle onto its base, a sharp rap sounded at the front door. I glanced towards it.

"I expect that'll be the police."

Damian grinned. "You are joking, aren't you? You don't really think I'm on the run."

"No, it really is the police. They've come to interview me after the mayhem at the fireworks party last night. I don't know why you're looking so surprised, Damian. You told me when I was leaving Frankfurt that English villages are rife with crime."

He did a double-take. "Yes, but I was only joking."

I stared at him for a moment, open-mouthed. "Oh God, yes, I knew that. Of course."

There was another knock at the door.

"Now listen, Damian, I'd better go and let him in. Make yourself a cup of tea while I talk to the policeman. There's bread there for toast. And keep the door closed. I may be some time."

Half an hour later, having completed my official statement, I dispatched Bob, our village bobby, with a friendly wave. He'd have a long day gathering more witness statements, as most of the village had been at the party.

Returning to the kitchen, I found Damian halfway through the packet of special shortbread I kept for Joshua's visits. He was on his third cup of tea, judging by the trio of soggy teabags basking in brown pools on the draining board, but he hadn't thought to make one for me. He was drinking out of my favourite mug, too.

Pointedly I took a fresh cup from the cupboard and threw in a teabag so crossly that it missed the cup entirely and landed on the floor. I said nothing.

Damian, resting his muddy shoes comfortably on the chair opposite him, displayed his most winning smile, forgetting I had long been immune. "So, where were we? About my new job."

It was always about him. Even though I'd just been interviewed by a policeman, it didn't occur to him to ask why. I could have been a murder suspect, for all he knew. Some people never change.

"The Wendlebury Barrow Players," he was saying. "I'm the new director of the Wendlebury Barrow Players."

"They're called the Wendlebury Players. Drop the Barrow. And that's not a job, that's a hobby."

He leaned his chair back on two legs.

"Really, Sophie, it's time you got over your petty snobbishness. Just because theatre actors don't earn as much as movie stars doesn't diminish their value to civilised society. And director is as high a position as you can get."

"No, Damian. With the Players, the post is definitely a hobby, like dominoes and darts and bridge. They're an amateur company that meets for a couple of hours once a week after work. They stage two shows a year, for a few nights only. The cast have day jobs, including the director. The last director was a teacher, like me. That's how he earned his keep."

"Oh." Damian crashed his chair back onto all four legs. "Oh well, it's still good experience. I only need a temporary job anyway, to tide me over till our spring bookings. We're touring Spain at Easter, and rehearsals start in February."

I poured boiling water on my teabag and jabbed at it with a spoon to hasten the brewing process.

"Didn't you do any research before you accepted the post? And how did you even know about it anyway?"

When he took another biscuit, I picked up the packet, resealed it and put it away in the cupboard. Pushing his feet off the chair, I sat opposite him and clasped my hands on the table, feeling like a detective questioning a suspect.

"I saw the ad on your bookshop website," he said. "I thought you were hinting."

I cursed myself for posting him a bookmark from Hector's House when I got the job, wanting to show how well I was doing without him. He must have got the website address from there.

"And where and how do you think you're going to live, on no salary, between now and spring? Surely not in your van?"

Damian tapped the table. "No, right here, of course, with you." He reached across the table to cover my hands with his, batting his long blond eyelashes.

"Over my dead body!"

I snatched my hands away and put them on my lap. Undeterred, he slipped off his shoes and reached one foot across to rest on my thigh. When I dragged my chair back out of reach, his big blue eyes widened.

"But Sophie, I'm committed. Some bloke called Ian, one of the Wendlebury Players, emailed me to say I could start straight away. Don't you want me to help your beloved village?"

"I want you to behave like a responsible adult and go away. Did you even look at the Players' website before you agreed to join them? If you had, you'd have seen the post is completely unsuitable for you."

Damian shrugged. "Going online has been tricky since you left and took your laptop with you. In internet cafes, the clock's always ticking – you pay by the minute."

"Damian, don't try to pretend this is my fault. Why didn't you check on your smartphone?"

He stared out of the window into the back garden. "I lost it. Dropped it. It broke."

Then I thought I'd hit upon a certain deterrent. "Anyway, it's my script they're using. You said you would have to be desperate to use a play I'd written."

He stared at me with those dangerous Viking eyes. "Well, maybe I am."

4 Shortbread and Short Temper

Damian dropped his stare only when he was distracted by something stirring in the back garden. He turned and pointed out of the window.

"Look out, there's some old tramp coming up your garden path. Do you want me to chase him away for you? Shall I go out and thump him?"

I'd forgotten I'd promised my elderly neighbour Joshua a post-mortem of the fireworks party. I pointed sharply to the front door, and spoke in the tone of a dog owner ordering a recalcitrant hound to its basket.

"Damian, van!"

To my surprise, it worked. For an instant, I wondered whether if I'd been as assertive when we were together, I'd never have left him. No. I'd have killed him by now.

I watched him all the way to the front door, which, careless as ever, he failed to shut properly behind him. I darted out to lock it before opening the back door to welcome Joshua. Today my life seemed to have become a revolving door for men: I was on to my third of the day, and it wasn't even lunchtime.

I hoped Joshua's soothing presence would calm me down.

"Good morning, young Sophie." He crossed the kitchen slowly and took his usual place in the chair that I'd just vacated. "I trust your party went well."

I needed to gather my wits. "I'll tell you once I've made the tea."

It took a whole pot of tea (Joshua preferred his tea from a pot) to give him the edited highlights of the vicar's party, which he enjoyed along with the rest of the shortbread. He then leaned forward on his stick to speak confidentially.

"So who is that dashing young adventurer who's been at my shortbread?"

I pursed my lips. Joshua might be old and infirm, but he never misses a trick. "Let's call him an unexpected ghost from my past."

"Not the Ghost of Christmas Past?" He chuckled. "Not Damian?"

"Yes, Damian. He thinks he's come to direct the nativity play."

"That's good news for the Players. They need a new director. Are the rehearsals going well?"

I realised talking about the play would divert Joshua from asking where I'd been when Damian arrived in the dead of night.

"The Players like the script. After they'd had their first read-through, the school staff will join them the following week. The children's rehearsals will be on Saturdays after that. They won't have any words to learn, we just need to block out their moves."

Joshua nodded his approval. "I shall look forward to seeing the results. The simple poetry of the nativity play is hard to beat."

I grimaced. "My script isn't exactly Shakespeare. To be honest, I'm a bit worried everyone will think it's dreadful."

He reached across the table and patted my hand. "Never go to meet trouble half way, my dear. It'll find you soon enough without your help."

5 The Professional Verdict

"You know your script is an absolute joke, don't you?"

Damian threw the dog-eared pages down on the kitchen table. I hadn't asked him to read it. After I'd let him back into the house following Joshua's departure, he'd just helped himself to my script, while I was upstairs changing out of my firework party clothes: a silk dress and thermal underwear. Hector had been chivalrous the night before, sweetly declaring "It's like playing Pass the Parcel."

I'd come downstairs now in an unflattering ski sweater and corduroy leggings. Not that Damian would have noticed if I was dressed as the back half of the pantomime horse. No, actually he would, but only to give me stage directions.

I stood at the foot of the stairs to keep my distance.

"I'm surprised you get the jokes, not knowing who is playing which part. If you lived here and knew everyone, as I do" – that was a bit of an exaggeration, but he wasn't to know – "you'd find them hilarious."

"No, no, I don't mean it's funny. I mean the whole script is a joke. And not in a good way. In any case, should you really have jokes in a religious play? It's like adding a song and dance routine to *King Lear*. As for working with children and animals, well, really—"

"The Players and the school staff are very taken with the concept," I said stiffly. "Bringing the schoolchildren and village drama group together will provide an invaluable educational experience. The Players needed a script to suit them. The children wanted a nativity play instead of a pantomime for a change. My script has saved the day for all of them."

Damian shot me a disparaging look. "And are any of them theatre professionals, as I am?"

To avoid answering, I busied myself clearing away the used mugs and biscuit crumbs. He got up to stand behind me as I washed up the mugs, putting his hands around my waist beneath the ski sweater.

"Damian, get off me!"

I wriggled out of his grasp, remaining as far away from him as possible while I dried them up.

"And my professional advice and expertise could save your little play from disaster."

He'd barely been an hour in my house, but already he was making me feel as if I'd just travelled back in time to the uncertain, undermined Sophie that I was when I'd moved to the village. This was a journey I had no wish to undertake. But nor did I want to lose face before my new friends by my play turning into a fiasco.

Damian returned to the table, picked up a pen, and began marking director's notes on my script.

6 The Would-be Lodger

Fancy a drink at The Bluebird at seven? H x.

Hector's text around noon was as welcome as a file inside a cake for a prisoner.

I'd have fancied anything at The Bluebird, including a wrestling match with a crocodile, rather than spend a moment longer in my cottage with Damian. Even after he'd had a long shower to freshen up, I felt as if his presence was polluting my new territory.

When I went to gather up the wet towels I knew he'd have left on the bathroom floor, I found him testing out my aunt's double bed – my bed, as it was now. I stood on the threshold to admonish him.

"Don't go getting ideas, Damian, this is my room."

He used his big blue eyes like a weapon. "But surely after all our years together, this little break doesn't change things between us?"

I threw the wettest towel at his head. "Damian, my moving to Wendlebury was not an interval between acts." I thought theatrical terms might make the message clear. "It was curtains for our relationship. Last bow. No encores. Ever."

He smirked. "Not even a quick matinee performance? A revival of a much-loved classic for old times' sake?"

I really wanted to beat him at his own game.

"Damian, that particular theatre has gone dark once and for all. The box office is closed. Boarded up. Show's over."

Some of my confidence was starting to seep back. "And besides, the role of Sophie's boyfriend has been recast. No further auditions necessary."

He heaved himself off the bed.

"So where am I supposed to sleep, then?"

"Where you usually do. In your van. Preferably somewhere far away on continental Europe."

He looked glum as he squeezed past me on to the landing. Then he paused and pointed into the spare room, so inviting with its faded sunshine yellow floral bedspread and matching curtains.

"What about in there? The decor's a bit twee, but I could always give it a makeover, if you like. I'm good at decorating."

I thought of all the happy summer nights I had spent in that room when I stayed with Auntie May in my school holidays. Not content with disrupting my present, now Damian was trampling on my past. I shook my head.

"Don't even think about it."

He shrugged and trudged back down the stairs. I found myself drifting into the spare room and lying down on the bed to think. When Damian turned on the television too loudly downstairs, I wrapped the eiderdown around me for comfort.

Waking up a little later, I wondered hazily why I was so tired and hungry. Then I remembered the night before. My broad smile was extinguished by the noise from downstairs, reminding me of Damian's presence.

Returning to the kitchen, I made us each a toasted sandwich for a late lunch, then curled up on my bed with

Sherlock Holmes, counting down the minutes until it was Hector o'clock.

7 Escape to the Bluebird

"Don't worry, he's not staying," I reassured Hector over a shared bottle of Pinot Grigio.

"Not staying with you, or not staying in the village?"

Hector, poker-faced, was fiddling with his beer mat, which was now fraying at the edges.

"Neither. I've said he can stay tonight to catch up on his sleep after his long drive from Germany. Do you know how many accidents are caused by driving while you're tired? Damian quoted me some horrendous figures."

Hector said nothing, but ripped the beermat in two.

"And I have told him about us. You and me. So I'm not giving him any false hopes." I reached across the table to put the remnants of the beermat in an empty glass out of harm's way. "And that he's got to sleep in the van."

Hector brightened a little. "Good."

I smiled reassuringly. "Honestly, you've got nothing to worry about. He's no competition, in any respect." I stared at him until he looked into my eyes, then he bucked up.

"OK, Sophie, I'll take your word for it."

I tried to steer our conversation on to more comfortable ground. "So how were your parents?"

"Oh fine, same as usual. You know."

I didn't know. I'd not yet met them. I pressed him for details. "So what did you do with them all day?"

"Oh, the usual. Ate lunch, drank tea, went for a walk, looked at old photos, played cards. Family stuff."

His description was so vague that for a moment I wondered whether he had been with another woman. I tried a different tack.

"What's Clevedon like? I've never been there."

"There are worse places to visit your parents."

"What, you mean like prison?" I thought making him laugh might ease the tension, but it just sent him off at a tangent.

"Did you have your police interview today? I'm having mine tomorrow."

I hadn't intended to bring up that topic tonight. We'd had more than our fair share of crime in the village since I'd moved here, and I wanted to put this latest episode behind me as quickly as possible.

"Yes. But let's not talk about that now. Let's talk about things to look forward to. Like Christmas. When does the festive season really kick off in Wendlebury? I'm looking forward to my first village Christmas."

Hector's shoulders relaxed a little. "I'm quite traditional. I don't do anything Christmassy in the bookshop till after Remembrance Day."

I tried not to look disappointed. "I bet Carol goes to town with festive decorations for the village shop, doesn't she? She put so much time and effort into Halloween."

Hector put down his glass. "Then prepare to be surprised. She doesn't do much at all for Christmas, beyond providing for her customers' seasonal grocery needs. She doesn't even put up decorations."

I traced my forefinger around the rim of my empty wineglass.

"You're right, I am surprised. Carol is the last person I'd expect to be a Scrooge. Don't tell me she keeps her shop open on Christmas Day?"

Hector reached for the wine bottle to replenish our glasses. "No, she's not quite that bad. And it's not fair to call her a Scrooge. Her motives aren't meanness or profit. She's simply not keen on Christmas."

I frowned. "I didn't know that. I hope it won't stop her from making the costumes for my nativity play." Carol was the Players' wardrobe mistress. I'd rather taken her cooperation for granted. I took a sip of wine, then held the chilly glass to my cheek to cool it. "Maybe I should have let the school stick with its usual pantomime."

"It's not the religious element that puts her off. Remember, she is a churchgoer."

Hector held the wine bottle up to the light to see how much we had left, then set it down on a fresh beermat and gazed at me, as if wondering whether to share a confidence.

"The thing is – and please don't tell Carol I've told you – she had a traumatic event one Christmas. I think that's spoiled it for her ever since."

My eyes widened. This sounded juicy. "Poor Carol. You mean like a break-in at her shop? An armed raid?"

Hector shook his head and looked away. "No, much worse than that – in her terms, at least." He lowered his voice and leaned forward. "One Christmas Eve, when she was about twenty, she ran away with someone much older than herself. She knew her parents would disapprove, but he'd turned her head."

I clapped my hands over my mouth. "Who was he? A stranger in town?"

Hector smiled wanly. "Believe it or not, someone from the village. But no-one you know. He never returned. She came back alone. I was only little at the time, so it passed me by, but my mum was close friends with Carol's mum, and she told me about it years later."

"What was he like?"

"A complete reprobate. Arrogant, lazy and conceited, my mum said. He persuaded her to go off in his van, telling her he had jobs fixed up for them both down in Brighton, but he'd made that up."

It was hard to associate such foolish behaviour with the down-to-earth Carol that I knew.

"Did her parents report her missing? Did they call the police?"

"No point," said Hector. "She was over the age of consent, and she had left a note making it clear she'd gone of her own free will. There was nothing they could do, except keep her bedroom ready and hope she might return."

"Which she did?"

Hector nodded. "Eventually. But she kept them waiting a whole year. Poor souls – their only child, too."

As an only child myself, I understood.

"When she came back, she had nothing but what she was standing up in. She was too ashamed to come back at first, so when her boyfriend abandoned her a couple of months after they left, she took refuge in a homeless shelter and got a job with a room in some seedy bar."

"How awful." I put down my glass.

"But the publican must have been a decent type, because he persuaded her to return home the following Christmas. Her parents welcomed her back, of course, but on Boxing Day her mother had a severe stroke, and was never really well again."

He gazed into the distance for a moment.

"And the rest you know – that she stayed nursing her mother and helping her father in the shop, till in time it was their turn to leave her."

"They ran away too?"

He pursed his lips.

"No, Sophie, they died."

"Goodness. No wonder she finds Christmas so difficult."

"So now you see why switching to a panto would serve no purpose at all."

"Just as well, as I'd never be able to write one of those."

"I could help you, if you like?"

I shot him a dubious look. "I shouldn't have thought it was your style either. Or is Hermione Minty hankering to play a pantomime dame?" Hermione Minty was the penname Hector used to write romantic novels, the profits of which secretly subsidised his bookshop. "Do you have panto experience?"

"Only that I've seen every school panto staged in the village for the last seven years. Which is about seven too many. Still, better a panto than a farce."

For a moment I thought he'd been speaking to Damian about my script, then I looked up to see his green eyes twinkling.

"Oh, Hector, you are a tease!"

He smiled. "I aim to please."

8 Dislodged

Always glad to return to work after the weekend, I was especially eager to leave my cottage that Monday before Damian surfaced from his van. To salve my conscience for making him sleep outside, I'd given him a spare key so that he could use my bathroom. I hoped he'd abandon his plan to direct the Players now he knew the post was unpaid, and instead head off to his parents' house, his Plan B bolt-hole till he returned to mainland Europe in February. With luck, he'd be gone before I got home from work, sparing us both any further unpleasantness.

I was therefore irritated when I popped down to the village shop later to find Damian deep in conversation with Carol. She was leaning coquettishly on the counter, lapping up his every word.

Damian turned to greet me as if he'd lived in the village all his life. "Oh, hello, Sophie. Carol and I were just chatting about costumes for our nativity play." So it was his play too now, was it? "She's got some brilliant ideas."

Carol beamed in appreciation. Her skills as a dressmaker were much admired in the village, but Damian must have been laying on the praise even thicker than she was used to.

She turned to me, pink-cheeked. "Damian's been telling me all about his touring theatre company. What an exciting and rewarding life, Sophie! I can't imagine how you could bear to leave it behind to move to Wendlebury."

I suppressed my impulse to put her straight. There was no point in crushing the pleasure she was deriving from Damian's honeyed words. She didn't have much other excitement in her life. I left them to it and headed down the aisle to the refrigerator for some milk, planning a swift exit.

Carol called after me, "You know, it will be such a thrill for the Players to have a professional detector for once, and the children too."

Smiling stiffly, I made a mental note to explain to Damian afterwards that Carol's choice of words was sometimes inexact.

"Unfortunately there's been a misunderstanding, Carol. Damian thought it was a paid post, and he needs to earn his keep. So he can't take the job after all. He's going to get seasonal retail work instead, or perhaps be a Christmas postman, while he's staying with his parents in Northampton. Aren't you, Damian?" I tested my new dog-trainer look on him. "I'm sure your parents will be glad to have you at home. Such a treat for them when you're usually abroad so much."

Carol paused to think for a moment. "Well, that's easily solved. He can come and stay with me till the play's over. I've got spare bedrooms, and I had been thinking of taking in lodgers. It seems a crime to have rooms standing empty when there are people needing them."

She gazed at Damian hopefully. He coughed, uncomfortable. "That's a kind offer, Carol, but I'm afraid

Sophie's right. I don't have the wherewithal to pay you rent."

Carol waved away his objection. "Oh, don't worry about rent. From what you've just been telling me about how good you are at making stage sets, it sounds as if we could come to a mutually beneficial arrangement. Instead of paying me rent, you could do some odd jobs in my house and shop. A spot of decorating, perhaps."

I fumbled for some change in my coat pocket. It didn't occur to me that Damian, who had never fixed a thing in any of my flats, would say yes.

His surprises were never the welcome sort.

"Thank you, Carol, you're on," he said, beaming. "That would fill the gap nicely for me. But only till the play's over. I'll be like Mary Poppins – I'll go when I'm no longer needed. Then I'll head up to my folks. So I'll be able to help you too, after all, Sophie. That's win-win, eh?"

I felt I'd won the booby prize.

"So if you tell me where your house is, Carol, I'll go and move my van there now."

Carol froze, her hand on the till to ring up my purchase.

"Your van, Damian?" Her face clouded for a moment, and I realised she must have been thinking about her Christmas misadventure long ago.

"My travelling theatre van, Carol." He made it sound more glamorous than it was.

She took my money and gave me my change. Then, on a white paper bag torn from the bunch hanging by a string from a nail next to the till, she scribbled down her address, sketched a street map with the effortless lines of someone good at art, and handed it to Damian. As he strode out of the shop, studying the route, she was positively quivering.

When the door swung closed behind him, she emitted a little sigh of satisfaction. "He's very handsome, isn't he? It must have been hard for you to break up with him."

I forced a smile. "That's probably why it took me seven years."

"You did what?"

I thought it better to tell Hector rather than let him find out from someone else about Damian's new arrangement.

"It's not my fault. I didn't do anything. They decided it between themselves. And at least it means I needn't put him up."

Hector scowled. "He'll break Carol's heart. You do know that, don't you?"

I crossed to the tearoom to put the milk in the fridge.

"I don't think he'd do that on purpose. He's not setting out with that intention."

Hector sighed. "People seldom do." I realised with sadness that he was probably thinking of Celeste, my predecessor in his affections. She had left him for another woman and emigrated to Australia. Much as I would have preferred Damian to leave, I hoped his presence might buck up Hector's ideas about me.

Hector fixed his eyes on his keyboard and started to type very fast.

9 Test Driving the Nativity

"Look out, young Sophie, you've caught your fancy man red-handed with another woman!"

Sitting on the sofa nearest the door in the lounge bar of The Bluebird was Billy, the old man whom I'd got to know as a regular customer of Hector's House. He wasn't interested in books or reading, however, but in the illicit hooch that Hector slipped into his elevenses to keep him happy. Billy nodded towards a booth on the far side of the bar. There Hector was tucking into a steak dinner, his dining companion out of sight behind the high-backed bench seat. I slumped down beside Billy, who shouted across to Hector before I could stop him.

"Oi, Hector, aren't you going to introduce your ladylove to your dinner guest?"

I cringed some more, until Hector replied slightly guardedly, "Don't you remember, Billy? They've already met, on Saturday night at the fireworks party."

Hector beckoned me to his table, and I tried to saunter over casually as if I'd never suspected his date was anything other than family.

Katherine Blake, commonly known as Kate, was Hector's godmother. She'd just returned from a long holiday in Australia, which had begun before I'd moved to the village back in the summer. But she set down her fish knife and fork, held out her hands and hauled me down to kiss her on both cheeks like an old friend, rather than an acquaintance encountered only once at a crime scene.

"Sophie, my dear, I'm so pleased to see you again. I was just asking Hector why he didn't bring you along tonight."

I looked furtively at Hector for a clue. She seemed to have assumed our relationship was more established. I didn't yet rank as his constant companion, even if our third date had ended with breakfast. But Kate was unstoppable. "Hector's been telling me all about you, Sophie. Why don't you come and join us now?" She patted the seat beside her, then changed her mind. "Oh, but of course, you'll want to sit next to Hector. Budge up, Hector. Make room."

Shooting me an apologetic look, Hector shuffled along the bench seat obediently. I'd never seen anyone boss him about before. I remained standing.

"That's very kind of you, Kate, but I'm afraid I'm already spoken for tonight."

Kate shot Hector a look of mock horror. "You see, Hector, what did I tell you? I know what you're like. Hang back too much and you'll lose her."

As she turned to beckon to Donald, the publican, for an extra glass and a menu, Hector put his head in his hands.

"Beam me up, Scottie," he said in a low voice so only I could hear, and I laid my hand reassuringly on his shoulder.

Kate turned back to me, beaming. I was genuinely sorry to have to turn down her invitation.

"I really have got a prior engagement." Kate's face fell. "I'm meeting a girlfriend for a drink and a chat." I held up my script. "We're brainstorming about the nativity play I've written for the Wendlebury Players and the village school."

Kate took the script from my hands, although I hadn't offered it to her. "How wonderful. Much better than those tired old school pantomimes, don't you think, Hector?" She flicked through it too fast to read more than the odd sentence. "A new community-wide project. What a wonderful idea. I can see this becoming an annual village tradition."

Gently but firmly I took back my script, wishing I had her confidence in the production. "Well, let's wait and see how it goes first, shall we?"

Donald delivered the requested extra glass. Kate filled it from the bottle, passed it to me, and raised her own drink in a toast. "Here's to you, my dear, and all that you're bringing to Wendlebury." She glanced at Hector. "What a treat for dear Reverend Murray, too, just as he returns in time for Advent." Her trilling laughter, reminiscent of a slightly raucous tropical bird, probably went down well in Australia.

I heard the pub door open behind me, and I turned to see Ella, the village school's business manager who had become a good friend since I'd moved to the village. We often met at The Bluebird for a drink and a chat.

Alerted by Kate's laughter, Ella spotted us straight away and strode over cheerfully to join us.

"Hello, Kate, welcome back. I don't know – the lengths some people will go to in order to miss a school governors' meeting."

Kate rose to embrace Ella as warmly as she'd greeted me. "Ella, my dear, how lovely to see you." She noticed my script's twin peeking out of Ella's handbag. "Ah, so you're Sophie's mysterious friend, robbing me and Hector of her company tonight. Once I've caught up with my inbox, I shall email you to fix a date for my school assembly on Australia. I've got plenty of gorgeous photos to share with the children of all those strange Australian creatures - kangaroos, koalas, wombats. I'll use them to encourage the children to embrace and rejoice in difference in a sublimely subtle sermon against bullying. I thought I might also read them the Winnie the Pooh chapters about Kanga and Roo arriving in the Hundred Acre Wood."

Ella beamed. "I'm sure the headmistress will be delighted. I might even persuade the dinner ladies to do an Australian themed school dinner that day. Not sure what, though. Any suggestions?"

"Emu steak and Fosters?" said Hector.

"Hector!" Kate slapped his hand playfully. "That's exactly the kind of stereotype I want to avoid."

Ella laughed.

"Maybe the children's English lessons that day could be about Australian dialect," I said tentatively, wanting to be part of this cosy clique.

Kate clapped her hands. "What fun! What a team! My word, we're on fire tonight."

Ella grinned. "Good to have you back, cobber. The school governors' meetings aren't half as lively without you. Now, come on, Sophie, Hector's made me thirsty for a lager."

As Ella and I headed for the bar, I heard Kate say in a stage whisper, "Talented as well as beautiful. You want to hang on to her, Hector. She's divine." I didn't hear Hector's reply.

Ella leaned comfortably on the bar, looking back towards Hector's table. "She's a force of nature, that Kate, don't you think? The kids love her, though. Even the naughty ones."

Once we'd got our drinks, I steered us towards the furthest table from Hector and laid my copy of the script in front of me.

"So, are you still sure we're doing the right thing, using my script? You're not just being kind to me? You haven't had second thoughts since rereading it?"

Ella pulled her copy out of her bag and opened it at the first page, which to my relief showed only a couple of tiny edits. I'd half-expected to see it covered in red ink with "Must try harder" scrawled across the title page.

"It's fine, Sophie. Stop worrying. You've got a real ear for dialogue, and you've got the measure of the community. They'll love it."

I wasn't so easily reassured. "You don't think I've taken too many liberties with the basic story?"

"Nah. Not compared to what the kids will take themselves. It's sweet, respectful and touching. Having naturalistic dialogue in there, instead of stagey dramatic proclamations, makes it more meaningful to modern children. And even though you're restricting the dialogue to the adults, you've given the kids plenty of carols to sing to vent their high spirits."

"I did wonder whether they'd be unhappy about that, being used to having lines in the school pantomime."

Ella shook her head. "I wouldn't worry. As long as they're on stage in front of their parents in fancy costumes, they'll be happy. But you know what they say."

"No, what?"

"Never work with children and animals. So don't give the donkey any dialogue either."

As I forced a feeble grin, our conversation was interrupted by a raucous group emerging from the public bar.

Ella nodded towards the gaggle of men. "Gosh, who's that handsome stranger in town?"

With a sinking feeling, I swung round to see Damian at the centre of the bunch, being clapped on the shoulder by a grinning Ian, one of my friends from the Wendlebury Players.

"You'll have to join the pub darts team after that performance, mate," Ian was saying as they headed for the bar. I ducked down over my script as if studying it intently, hoping my hair falling across my face might provide a curtain of invisibility. As the men seethed past us, a large hand reached out to pat me roughly on the head. I didn't need to look to know it was Damian's.

"Gosh, you might be in there, Sophie," hissed Ella excitedly once they'd gone past. "Hector'd better look out – he's got competition."

"He most certainly has not." I explained to Ella about Damian's surprise reappearance. She was all sympathy, especially when she'd established Damian was single. She patted her hair into place.

"You'll have to fight Carol for him, mind. He's her new lodger." I told Ella about his deal with Carol and the Players. She flexed her arm muscles, Popeye style.

I tapped my script to return to the reason for our meeting.

By the time Hector came over to kiss me goodnight before escorting his godmother home, I was feeling more reconciled to the latest developments in the Damian saga. Then I caught a snippet of their conversation in the street as they passed by the open window. Kate's voice cut flute-like through the evening mist.

"Of course, the biggest highlight of the trip was spending time with my great-godchild."

Great-godchild? Of course! She'd just been to Australia, where Celeste, Hector's ex, had gone to live after their break-up. They must have had a child that Hector hadn't told me about. So that was why he hadn't wanted me to visit his parents' house on Sunday. They'd have photos of the baby in pride of place.

His baggage was much bigger than he'd confessed to me. And it wasn't going to go away.

10 A Medieval Mystery

By the time I arrived at Hector's House next morning, I'd worked myself into a bit of a state. The night before, I'd been having nightmares about Hector emigrating to Australia, taking the bookshop with him and changing the stock exclusively to board books for babies.

So I was glad to find it was business as usual when I arrived to see him emptying a box of First World War poetry and history books on to the central display table. Remembrance Day was our final theme before the onslaught of Christmas, when there'd be no escaping the focus on the nativity.

"Could you add these poppies to the window display please, sweetheart? Carol crocheted them for us over the weekend."

He flattened the emptied cardboard box and took it out to the stockroom.

Then Damian walked in, closely behind the school-run mums. I ignored him, heading over to the tearoom to serve the ladies their morning coffee. Chatting to them as if he wasn't there, I tried at the same time to tune in to the conversation at the main counter between Damian and Hector.

"Can you point me in the direction of your drama section, please?" Damian was saying. "I'm looking for a particular script." I cringed. I knew our drama range was tiny, but that was not unreasonable, given that the only drama books our customers ever requested were actors' life stories and gift editions of Shakespeare.

As I poured the frothed milk on to some cappuccinos, one of the mums came up to the cake counter and said in a low voice, "Who's that, Sophie? Is he a regular?"

I said what I wanted to believe. "No, he's just passing through."

"Shame, because he's a bit fit," she said. "A sight for sore eyes at this time of the morning."

Yes, but not fit for purpose as a boyfriend, I thought bitterly.

As I delivered the cappuccinos to her table, she was saying to her friends, "He'd look good in one of those Nordic noir sweaters."

"I'm thinking of getting my Dave one of those for Christmas," said another mum. "Though it won't look quite the same on him."

"My Paul lives in fleeces," said another.

"You make him sound like a sheep," said the first.

The woman nodded. "Same sort of build. Barrel of a body on spindly legs. Quite cuddly, though."

I tuned out when Damian returned to the shop counter.

"I couldn't find what I was looking for," he said to Hector abruptly. "There's not much there. Do you have any more scripts tucked away anywhere – misfiled, perhaps?"

Hector, who prided himself on being orderly, shook his head. I felt awkward on Hector's behalf. It can't have been easy to have to serve his romantic predecessor. I'd never have coped with Celeste as a customer. But Hector managed to remain civil. After all, a customer was a customer, and Damian's money was as good as the next person's.

"If you tell me exactly what you're looking for, perhaps I can be more helpful?"

Damian glanced in my direction, presumably to check whether I was listening. I averted my gaze, pretending to be busy filling china pots with cutlery. The mums had fallen silent to eat cake, so I could hear him better than he might have realised.

"I'm after the York Mystery Plays," said Damian. "I don't mind what format or edition. But I need them for tomorrow."

Hector looked hopeful. "Why, are you planning to leave town?"

I crossed my fingers.

Damian gave a short laugh. "Town? You've got delusions of grandeur, haven't you? This is only a little village. No, it's for the Wendlebury Barrow Players. They need a Christmas play, and I thought the medieval scripts would be spot on."

"I thought they'd already chosen their play?"

I was grateful for Hector's diplomacy.

"No, not really. I mean, Sophie's had a stab at writing one, but it's hardly professional standard. If I'm going to direct it, I'll want decent material."

Hector pulled the order book out from under the counter.

"You do know it's a very small company, don't you?" he asked, opening the book at the next blank page. "Just five women and one man? The Mystery Plays have huge casts."

Damian had never taken kindly to having his judgment challenged. "But there'll be plenty of extras from the village school."

41

Hector nodded towards the play table in the corner of the tearoom, where a couple of pre-school children were amusing themselves with robust board books. "You do realise it's a primary school, don't you? There's only so much stage direction a four-year-old will take."

Damian watched disdainfully as a little boy aged about three poked his left forefinger through a hole in *The Very Hungry Caterpillar* board book while burying his right forefinger up his nose.

"That doesn't matter, because the adults will have all the dialogue." He stroked his chin thoughtfully. "That gorgeous Middle English language rolls around the mouth so beautifully. It's a joy to perform."

At that point a girl of about two produced a half-sucked sugar lump from her mouth and held it up with the pride and wonder of a conjuror extracting a hidden egg.

Hector suppressed a knowing smile.

"But perhaps a little beyond the comprehension of the under-twelves?"

Damian scowled. "Listen, I'm a professional theatre director, so kindly leave the choice of material to me. Just order me a copy of the York Mystery Plays. You do your job, and I'll do mine."

As if to offset his rudeness, he flashed a white-toothed smile. A couple of the mums sighed wistfully.

Hector typed a quick search into the computer. "I can get you a second-hand edition in for tomorrow morning. I don't suppose it matters if it's used? It's not as if the words will have changed between print runs."

Damian gave an easy laugh, relaxing now that he'd got Hector to do his bidding. "Perfect. I need it for their meeting tomorrow night." He patted his pockets. "Oh, I'm sorry, I seem to have left my wallet at my digs." Digs.

As if Carol was a regular source of accommodation for itinerant thespians. "Any chance you could put it on Sophie's account for me?" He pointed vaguely in my direction, as if Hector might not know who I was. "Sophie and I are old friends. Our relationship goes back a very long way. Doesn't it, Sophie?"

"Rather too long, if you ask me," I said in the sweetest tone I could muster. I resented being portrayed as more Damian's than Hector's. "As does your running tab. I suppose next you'll be wanting to take advantage of my staff discount."

Damian perked up. "Ooh, can I? Thanks."

Hector was gripping the edge of the counter hard enough to turn his knuckles white.

"Don't worry, cash on collection tomorrow will do fine. If you don't mind getting your change in our local currency? Being that we're just a village, rather than a town."

Damian looked as surprised as I felt. "If that's the done thing around here. Of course, I'm used to doing everything in Euros these days." He glanced over to the mums to see whether any of them were impressed.

Hector extracted a small gold-coloured coin from a glass goldfish bowl behind the counter.

"Have you not yet encountered the Wendlebury pound?" He held the coin tantalisingly at eye level, just out of Damian's reach. Damian stared at it, reminding me of Jack being persuaded to trade his mother's cow for magic beans. Perhaps I should have written a panto after all.

Just then one of the toddlers pottered over to Hector with outstretched hands.

"Please may I 'ave one too, 'ector?"

Hector bent down and held it out kindly. "Of course you can, Ethan. But let Mummy unwrap it before you put it in your mouth." He grabbed another two chocolate coins and took them over to the Very Hungry Caterpillar fan and the sugar lump conjuror. "Here you go, you'd better have one each, so it's fair. Is that OK, Mummies?" He stood up straight and smiled winningly at the mums. "Left over from Halloween the other night. I'd over-catered for the callers, so I thought I'd bring the leftovers down for good children in the shop."

He'll make a lovely daddy one day, I thought, forgetting for a blissful moment that he already had.

Returning to the counter, Hector smiled coolly at Damian.

"OK, I get the message," he said crossly. "I'll pay tomorrow. How much?"

"To you, fifteen quid."

Flinching, Damian was about to leave when he remembered his audience. He turned back to give a little wave in the direction of the tearoom. "Bye, ladies. See you at my show, perhaps?"

His show? I'd forgotten just how arrogant he was. As the door closed behind him, one of the mums gave a low whistle.

"He's a handsome devil, isn't he?" The others nodded, gazing in silence at the door.

Hector, meanwhile, was chatting to the chocolatey toddlers about their board books. He probably appreciated their superior manners.

11 The Playwright's Audition

Having supplied Damian with the promised second-hand edition of the York Mystery Plays the next day, Hector said no more about their exchange. But he did invite me to come up to his flat for a nightcap after the Players' meeting that evening. At first I assumed his prime reason was to get the lowdown on the Players' response to Damian's suggested script change, but then I wondered whether "nightcap" might also be a euphemism for a sleepover. I stashed a toothbrush and a change of underwear at the bottom of my handbag before setting off for the Village Hall, just in case.

I'd meant to get to the Players' meeting early to upstage Damian, but spent too long getting ready. Having changed my clothes twice in the hope of looking more like an experienced playwright, I was the last to arrive. By the time I reached the hall, Damian was already holding court, regaling the other seven with some winning theatrical anecdote, no doubt having cast himself as its leading man.

Seven? I counted again. Since Linda's murder back in the summer, the company had been down to six. Then I realised the seventh person was Carol.

As wardrobe mistress, Carol didn't usually attend early rehearsals, and given her aversion to Christmas, I hadn't expected her to be there tonight. Damian's presence must have been an irresistible draw.

Mary spotted me and waved me over.

"Hi, Sophie, good to see you. We can't wait to start rehearsing your new play."

Before I sat down, I pulled their photocopies of my script out of my bag. My knickers, caught up on one of the bulldog clips holding the scripts together, fell out on to the floor. I hoped no-one saw.

I distributed the scripts to their eagerly outstretched hands. Damian's remained clasped around the small blue hardback book on his lap. I gave his copy to Carol instead.

"Of course, you've already seen it," I said to him pointedly.

He shot me a challenging stare, and moved his chair a couple of inches closer to Carol's. "That's OK, Sophie, I'll share Carol's." Carol squealed with pleasure.

"I wrote each part specifically with one of you in mind," I explained. "Mary, you're Mary. I thought that would be less confusing for the children."

"How lovely. I've always wanted to be Mary."

Damian looked at her as if she was simple.

"Ian, you're Joseph. I know you were hoping for a title role in the next production, but just think of this part as God's handyman, and that's pretty important."

Ian looked pleased. Pulling a highlighter pen out of his pocket, he started to search for his lines.

"Sally, I thought you'd be a terrific head shepherd, as I know the children will follow you anywhere." I'd seen Sally in action at the school as playground supervisor. "By process of elimination, the rest of you are the wise men. I'm sure Carol will run up some wonderful costumes for you."

To my relief, Carol nodded eagerly. "I'm thinking lots of brocade, shiny chintz and thick velvet, to hang well and rustle as you move. I've got some great materials in my trunk of old curtains. They'll be a fabulous contrast to the simple cottons and linens of the other characters."

"Don't forget the tea-towels on their heads." Although Damian's tone was sarcastic, Carol noted it on her script.

"The school staff playing the other parts won't be joining us till next week's meeting," I said, taking charge. "But shall we have a read-through of your parts now?"

Damian held up his hand to intervene. "Just a moment, folks. Before we go any further, I propose we step back to consider whether we've got the right script."

Ian flipped back to the title page. "Yes, it's definitely Sophie's nativity play."

Damian held up his little blue book. "Ah, but have you ever considered a more traditional approach?"

"A more traditional approach? You can't get much more traditional than a nativity play. I hope you're not going to suggest a pantomime." Mary was ready to defend her longed-for chance to play the Blessed Virgin against any competition.

Damian tapped his book. "Same story, but with a more poetic script. The ancient medieval mystery plays have been staged for vast audiences all over the country for centuries. Filled with beautiful language, they provide the perfect vehicle to bring the traditional Christmas story to the masses."

"Vehicles? We don't want to perform our play in the street," said Sally, frowning. "And at this time of year, we want to be indoors in the warm."

Damian looked arch. "Ah, you may jest." It was clear from Sally's expression that she did not. "But I'm not proposing we perform the play on carts pulled around town, as they did in medieval times. We'll give ours on stage, indoors, for the sake of convenience. That's easy enough."

"But a mystery play?" said Ian. "That's hardly in keeping with the spirit of Christmas. I know they always put an Agatha Christie on telly, but I don't think it's appropriate to have a murder mystery as our first joint drama venture with the school. Does the audience have to guess whodunnit? Is it a shepherd or a king?"

"Not much mystery there," said Mary. "It's obvious the baddie is going to be Herod, ordering all the under-twos dead. That would give the children nightmares."

"Especially the under-twos," said Sally. "And their parents."

"Not that sort of mystery," said Damian sharply. "Of course there's no murder in the Bible, is there?"

Ian raised his eyebrows. "Well, there's the crucifixion, for a start."

Damian waved his comment aside. "In this context, the word mystery is a corruption of maisterye, the old term for a tradesmen's guild. Each guild would stage an episode of the story." He opened his book at random. "So you see, here we've got the Chandlers' Guild responsible for the shepherds, the Goldsmiths for the Kings and so on. Pass the book round, and you'll see it's perfect."

He stood up, holding the open book at arm's length, and declaimed a few lines, other arm flung out, channelling his inner Kenneth Branagh.

"Ego sum Alpha et O, Vita Via,
Veritas, Primus et Novissimus.
I am gracious and great, God without beginning;

I am maker unmade, and all might is in me.
I am life and way unto weal winning;
I am foremost and first; as I bid shall it be.
I am maker unmade, and most high in might,
And aye shall be endless, and nought is but I'."

Always the egotist. Then he handed the book to Mary, and sat down again. She flicked through to find some of her own potential lines and read them aloud woodenly.

"'Alas, what ails that fiend,
That through wild ways makes us to went?
He does great sin;
From kith and kin
He makes us flee'."

She bit her lip anxiously. "Oh my goodness, what a mouthful."

"That's alliteration," explained Damian. "A poetic device. You probably don't come across it much in your work."

"No, I'm a nuclear physicist," said Mary tersely. The others sniggered, except Carol.

As the book was passed round the circle, it emerged the Players were less than keen.

"'Some marvel surely does it mean, that we shall see'," read Ian. "That sounds like something Yoda might say. And this sounds like something out of a panto: 'Ah sirs! Foresight what shall I say? Where is our sign? I see it not.' We expressly didn't want panto." He continued:

"'Hail! Food that they folk all fully may feed.
Hail! Flower fairest that never shall fade.
Hail! Son that is sent of this same seed.

That shall save us from sin that our sires made
And since thou shalt sit to be deeming,
To hell or to heaven to have us,
Incense to thy service is seeming.
Lord, see to thy servants and save us.""

"Ooh no, tongue-twister alert," said Sally reproachfully.

The others murmured their agreement.

When Damian, realising he was losing ground, turned to me with an appealing look, I saw my chance to seize the moral high ground.

"Well, Damian, thank you very much for your thoughtfulness and consideration in bringing your little book along, but I think the Players have made their choice clear. Still, I'm sure you'll do a wonderful job with my script instead."

Ian looked up from his copy, which he'd been studying while I was speaking. "Cracking job, Sophie. This dialogue is really natural. We'll have no trouble learning these lines."

The others nodded appreciatively.

"Plus of course your script will be free of charge, won't it?" put in Mary, the group's treasurer. "I mean, there won't be any royalties or licence fee to pay, will there?"

Damian waved his book again in defiance. "Nor would there be copyright on a medieval play."

"No, but that book looks expensive. How much did that set you back?"

"Fifteen quid."

"Well, then, I rest my case. Now, let's just all read Sophie's script through in our heads first, then grab a nice cup of coffee, and then have a proper read-through of the whole thing."

I beamed. "Thanks, folks. I'll put the kettle on." I passed my copy of my script to Damian. "Here, you can refresh your memory. Enjoy."

Carol, with no lines to read, came out to the kitchen with me to help with the coffees. With the serving hatch still closed, our conversation could not be overheard by the others.

"Thanks for the introduction to Damian, Sophie," she began, filling the kettle. I sensed she was bursting with the need to talk about him. "He's been a godsend. He's already fixed my back bedroom window and replaced all the spent light bulbs. And he got my wifi running faster. I forget how many millipedes per second he said it is now, but it's very, very fast. Tomorrow he's going to paint my bathroom."

"I'm glad he's making himself useful," I said, which was true. I spooned coffee into nine mugs.

"He's good company too. I feel I can really talk to him." That surprised me. I'd always found Damian a terrible listener. She produced a pint of milk from the basket she'd brought with her from the shop, and opened the cardboard box of sugar lumps. "Even about the most sensitive of subjects. Things I find it difficult to talk about to other people."

Given that I'd never found Carol anything less than garrulous, I wondered what on earth she could be telling Damian that she'd never told me.

12 A Traditional Nightcap

"I'm pleased to see you too, Sophie." Hector steadied himself against the door frame as I threw my arms round his neck. "Rehearsal go well, did it?"

When I released him, he closed the front door and followed me up the stairs to his flat.

"Yes! They hated Damian's idea and loved my script. The read-through was brilliant. It's going to be fantastic."

I hung my coat and scarf on the wall pegs and arranged my boots neatly on the floor beneath them.

"Steady on, early days yet. You've still got those animals and children to factor in."

I tutted. "Why does everyone keep saying that? It's not as if you can have a nativity play without them."

I sank down into one of the comfy leather wingback chairs that stood sentry either side of the blazing log fire.

"True," said Hector. "But not all directors cast live animals. How did Damian take their decision?"

I gladly accepted the glass of brandy he put into my hand. Holding it up to the firelight, I admired the colour, as rich as amber but without the fossilised insects.

"He didn't have much choice. They didn't hold back any punches. Mary even took him to task for spending £15 on his book."

Hector settled companionably into the armchair opposite, stretched his stockinged feet out to touch mine, and flashed me a mischievous smile. "Ah, about that book. I've got a confession to make. It cost me 50p at a flea market years ago."

I swirled the brandy round the glass, watching it form a little whirlpool. I wondered whether it would go in the other direction in Australia.

"Gosh, what are the chances of you just happening to have a copy of an obscure drama book like that lying about your flat?"

Hector chuckled. "Quite high, actually. I've never told you this before, but I pick up vintage books at car boot sales on Sundays, and sell them at a profit on the internet. I've got shelves and shelves of them in my spare bedroom." He jabbed his thumb over his shoulder towards the room behind him. "You can have a browse if you like."

So that's what he did with his parents on Sundays.

I did a quick bit of mental arithmetic. "So that's a 1,500% mark-up then?"

"Which probably makes him my most profitable customer of the year."

I paused to savour the thought. "By the way, is Mary really a nuclear physicist?"

"What? No, she works in a pet shop in Slate Green." He laughed when I told him my reason for asking. "Stop it, you're starting to make me feel sorry for Damian, and I don't want to."

"Can I look at your second-hand book collection now?" I thought it might give me more insight into his life outside of work.

"Of course."

All four walls were covered, floor to ceiling, with crowded bookshelves, the rows of vintage volumes only occasionally broken up by family photos and curios.

I pounced on a silver frame with two oval pictures showing a baby, thinking it must be Hector's and Celeste's. In one, the baby was gazing adoringly into the eyes of a beautiful young woman. Was this Celeste? If so, she must be into vintage clothes.

When I observed that the man cuddling the baby in the second photo looked very much like Hector, but with straight hair, I realised the couple must be Hector's parents, and the baby was Hector himself. No wonder the colours were a bit faded. False alarm.

For a moment, I felt sorry for Celeste's baby, growing up on the other side of the world from his father. I hoped Kate had spoiled him while she was there. Or was he a her? I didn't know.

A low cough alerted me to Hector leaning against the door frame, arms folded, head on one side.

"None of the books to your taste, Sophie?" Hastily I shoved the photos back where I'd found them.

"There's quite a selection here," I said, pulling the nearest book off the shelf at random. It fell open at a grisly diagram of a dissected eyeball. I snapped it shut and returned it to the shelf.

"Well, if there are any you want to borrow, help yourself. Or if you'd like recommendations, just say."

"Have you got a copy of Dickens' *A Christmas Carol*, please?"

Knowing that was his favourite Christmas book, I thought that request would please him.

He went straight to the slim red volume, its spine tooled in faded gold. "With the original illustrations by John Leech," he said proudly, offering it to me.

I took the book back to my comfortable fireside chair and cradled the warm brandy glass in my hand.

"I do appreciate your encouraging me to read more widely. I've read so many books since I started working at Hector's House. Most of them have been outside my comfort zone, but I have enjoyed them. I'm sure it's been good for me."

"I know. And I also know what you mean about appreciating encouragement."

With a twinkle in his eye, he nodded towards my handbag, which I'd slung on the floor beside my chair. I looked down to discover that my bag had fallen over, spilling its contents across his shag-pile rug. Nestling down on my white lace knickers, my toothbrush was glinting in the flickering firelight.

"Well, when you said nightcap, I wasn't sure—"

"My turn to thank you, I think," he said softly, raising his glass to me.

13 We Will Remember Them

"Before you do anything else this morning, you'd better go home and get a less brightly coloured sweater."

Sitting at a high stool at the breakfast bar in the small kitchen of Hector's flat, I was swinging my legs as if I didn't have a care in the world. I looked down quickly.

"Why, have I dropped yoghurt on it?" I couldn't see any. "I might get away with it. It's pretty much the same colour, raspberry."

Hector's mouth twitched. "No, you twit, what's today's date?" He pointed to a beautifully illustrated wall calendar from the Literally Gifted selection. The poem of the month was by Keats. I read the first stanza.

"What, seasons of mists and mellow fruitfulness? Are you saying I should be more autumnal? I suppose raspberry is a summer fruit."

He tapped the date. "No, more sombre. It's Remembrance Day."

"Oh." I was taken aback. "I never knew there was a dress code."

His brow furrowed for a moment, then relaxed.

"Sorry, Sophie, I was forgetting you're so new to the village. You won't know what we do here on Remembrance Day."

"Not that new," I objected. "I've been here nearly six months."

"That might not seem new in Earth years, but in Wendlebury terms, you moved in yesterday. What you don't know is that when Remembrance Day falls on a school day, everyone in the village goes up to join the children in two minutes' silence. I always shut the shop and go. I wouldn't serve anyone if they came in then anyway."

I glanced at the clock. "Please may I borrow one of your sweaters, to save going home to change?"

He looked at his watch. "If it means you will be on time for work for once."

I smirked. "People will talk!"

He chuckled. "They'll do that anyway. Besides, it's not as if my name's emblazoned across the chest of my sweaters. Help yourself, and I'll meet you downstairs in the shop."

He jumped down from his stool and came over to give me a quick kiss before we resumed our dutiful daytime personae of mere colleagues. We'd agreed we shouldn't be seen hugging or kissing in the bookshop, but I liked the idea of secretly being embraced by Hector's sweater all day instead.

As I passed the main till, I slid a pound coin into the British Legion box and picked up a paper poppy to pin on to my charcoal-coloured top.

"Nice sweater, Sophie," said one of the early morning mums as I set a caramel latte in front of her. "Lovely fit."

"It's cashmere," I told her. "It's ever so cosy, but it feels like I'm wearing nothing at all."

As soon as the shop was empty, Hector asked in a low voice, "You are wearing something under it, aren't you, Sophie?"

I nodded. "Yes, of course."

"Oh, OK. Just wondered." He was looking a little feverish.

Mid-morning, as I was boxing up some returns in the stockroom, I heard Kate's distinctive voice trilling in the shop.

"Just on my way to school, Hector, darling. I trust you'll be coming, as usual?"

I heard Hector agree. "And Sophie too."

"Ah yes, Sophie. What have you done with her?"

It seemed polite to emerge at that point, although I was nervous of seeing her again since her inadvertent revelation about Celeste's baby.

She came over to give me her trademark double kiss, resting her hands lightly on my shoulders, made kitten-soft in the cashmere. She stood back to appraise the sweater.

"Why, Hector, you old dog, isn't that your sweater? The one I gave you last Christmas?"

She gave him a stagey wink before turning back to me. "I bet that's not the only way he's been keeping you warm, eh, Sophie? I'll see you both at school shortly."

As she marched out of the shop, Hector avoided meeting my eye and changed the subject.

"The vicar usually takes the services, but in his absence, she's standing in for him."

I frowned. "She seems a bit frisky to be standing in for a vicar."

He passed me my coat.

"You won't say that once you've met the Reverend Murray," he said, slipping on his own jacket. "Kate may be a loose cannon in adult company, but she knows where to draw the line with children. She'll hit just the right mark, you'll see."

We joined the queue to file into the back of the school hall. As at the Friday Celebration Service, chairs had been put out for the adults, while the children sat cross-legged on the floor. Teachers on chairs at the edge of the room kept an eye on their classes.

In the visitors' seats at the back, I spotted lots of familiar figures from the village, all smartly dressed in dark colours. Some surprised me with evidence of a military background that I didn't know about – Forces berets, medals. Even Billy was wearing what looked like an old regimental tie.

Kate, standing at the front of the hall, had apparently left her natural frivolity at the school gate. She led the simple, short proceedings impeccably, explaining the significance of the service in terms that even the youngest child could understand. Her words made me feel unworthy for my earlier thoughts about her.

Two older children holding wooden descant recorders went to stand beside her, and Kate said some prayers for those who had sacrificed their lives for others and for the serving military. She instructed everyone to stand. Then one of the recorder players sounded "The Last Post". Kate's timing was perfect. As the wall clock clicked round to the eleventh hour, we began two minutes' silence, which by some miracle even the youngest pupils managed to keep.

As the second hand reached the twelve for the second time, the headmistress Head Mrs Broom raised her arm and the second recorder player sounded the "Reveille".

Next a group of about twenty children filed up to stand in line, and in turn announced the name of a member of the military. Wondering why the names sounded familiar, I realised after a moment I'd seen them all on the village war memorial.

Kate's voice, as penetrating as a fingertip circling the rim of a crystal glass, completed the ceremony. "'Age shall not weary them, nor the years condemn. At the going down of the sun and in the morning, we will remember them'."

At the far corner of the room, one of the teachers hit "play" on the sound system to start a CD of "Toll for the Brave", so familiar from the national Remembrance Day commemorations that would be broadcast from the Cenotaph in Whitehall the following Sunday. Each class was signalled by the headmistress to file out, while the parents remained seated. Some of the older girls were hugging each other or holding hands, faces wet with tears. I hoped none of their names would ever be added to the war memorial.

As if reading my thoughts, Hector leaned over and whispered to me, "Each child who said a name is related to that person. Separated by several generations, but of the same blood, though so many of those serviceman never had the chance to have children of their own."

I slipped my hand into Hector's and he gave it a gentle squeeze. As the last class filed out, I became aware of a rustling in front of me. Carol, in huge dark glasses, was fumbling in a large black handbag for a fresh tissue. As the other adults got up to leave, Carol remained seated, so I let go of Hector's hand and lingered to make sure she was OK.

Hector hurried off to catch up with the man wearing the most medals. Together they strolled more slowly across the school playground towards the gate.

14 We Can Be Heroes

Carol lowered her sunglasses to reveal red eyes.

"I'm sorry, I didn't know you'd lost someone in the military." Casting my mind back to my history A Level, I realised the Falklands War would have taken place in her prime.

"Oh no, Sophie, I didn't. I just feel the pain of what others have lost. Those little children, their families." She stood up, and we began to walk to the door together. "Then I think of the young lads in the village who would be called up if there was another war today. Tommy Crowe, for example, wouldn't have to wait long for his papers. And your Hector."

I shivered.

Putting my arm around Carol's shoulders, I guided her gently across the playground, out into the High Street, towards the shops. Hector, well ahead of us, had already reopened the bookshop. As we reached Hector's House, I could see several of the school's guests taking seats in the tearoom. I was relieved when Hector called to me through the open door.

"You walk Carol back to the shop, Sophie. I'll do the teas till you get back."

Carol flashed him a damp smile of gratitude. As we continued up the High Street, she told me more about the village war dead, stories of heartrending tragedy and remarkable bravery, such as the farming family that lost all three sons on the Somme.

"Just because we're a little village doesn't mean we can't produce heroes," said Carol proudly. Then her voice became very small. "But, Sophie, do you know what? In a selfish way, I envy them their loss, because if there was a war tomorrow, I would have no-one to fear for. No husband, no sweetheart, no son to send off into battle."

I fumbled for something consoling to say. "I'm sure we won't have another war like the First or Second World Wars, Carol. War's different these days. With terrorism, anyone can be killed on the street, any time, anywhere in the world."

Cringing at my ineptitude, I was glad that Carol didn't take it amiss.

"Of course, I care about my friends and my customers and everyone in this village, but that's not really my point. My mum used to say she was glad I was a girl, so that I could never get called up to fight."

We stopped outside the village shop, where Damian was up a ladder cleaning the big plate glass window with a rag, whistling contentedly. Her hand on the door handle, Carol gazed up at him wistfully.

"You're lucky, Sophie. Some people spend their entire lives looking for the kind of love that would make them feel that way, but they never find it. I thought I had once, but—"

Damian looked down quickly, then back up at his task, and Carol clammed up. Following her through the door into the shop, I steered her round to the stool behind the counter and sat her down.

I wanted to ask more, but Damian, insensitive as ever, bashed hard on the window from outside, still up his ladder.

"Could you open this top window, Carol? Save me getting down. I want to clean right under the latch."

She blinked up at him tearfully, then stood up to do his bidding before turning back to me.

"I was always so sure when I was a child that I'd have lots of kids myself when I grew up. Of course, it's too late for that now. Still, I try to look on the bright side. At this rate, I will never be heartbroken. But I'll never give up looking for that special someone."

She gave me a watery smile, and I realised she considered the conversation closed. She glanced up at Damian.

"You know, Carol—" I hesitated, following her gaze, "—maybe you just keep looking in the wrong places."

The doorbell jangled – another unwelcome interruption, just as I thought we were getting somewhere. In marched a man in a white coat and matching hat carrying a blue plastic mesh tray of fancy cakes.

"Morning, ladies. Any chance of seeing the manager, please?"

I broke away from Carol and came back to the customer side of the counter.

"That'll be me," said Carol, getting up from her stool. "There is only me."

15 A Military Two-Step

By Monday lunchtime, the first snowflakes were falling – in our shop window, anyway.

"So what else do I need to know about the village Christmas?" I asked Hector as I glued a collection of starched lace doilies that he'd kept from his parents' antique shop for this purpose on to the glass.

Standing on a chair to reach the ceiling, Hector paused with a vintage wicker sleigh and reindeer in his hands.

"Ooh, it's one long sleigh ride from now till C-Day. Wendlebury doesn't do Christmas by halves. Apart from doing this window display, I don't rush to embrace the onslaught until absolutely necessary."

I hoped he wouldn't leave it too late. One of the things I was expecting to miss about life on continental Europe was the traditional Christmas market. No matter how Scrooge-like you were feeling, they'd give you an instant fix of festive spirit.

"Besides the church's Advent services, there's the school Christmas fair, the carol singing, the big Christmas tree on the village green, the plethora of lights that villagers put in their gardens and on their houses, and the official switch-on of the Christmas tree lights."

He suspended the model sleigh from the hooks in the bay window ceiling and stepped down from his chair to assess whether it was hanging straight.

"Here in Hector's House, a visit from Santa on the first Sunday in Advent kicks off our Christmas marketing campaign proper. We open every Sunday afternoon from then until Christmas, just long enough for a story, a coffee and a bit of gift-buying."

He stepped back up on to the chair.

"Sorry, Sophie, I should have thought to tell you that at your job interview."

I passed him the knitted Santa to tuck into the sleigh, and he positioned the leather reins in its tiny hands.

"I'm amazed that people in the village buy enough books to justify you opening seven days a week," I said.

Hector adjusted the leading reindeer.

"It's not just Wendlebury folk who come in. I get people from all around at this time of year, by reminding them on social media, and any other way possible, of how much more civilised it is to do their Christmas shopping here than in the madness of town."

"I don't blame them," I said. "I hate crowded shopping centres at the best of times."

"I also offer free gift-wrapping throughout December, and I put a pot of gold and silver pens in the tearoom to encourage people to stay and write their Christmas cards here while drinking our coffee and eating festive food. Hector's House – the one-stop Christmas present shop."

I liked the sound of that.

"What a good idea. You must feel really festive by the time Christmas actually comes around."

Anyone this thoughtful and inventive in the shop would be a wonderful companion for the Christmas holidays.

"Yes, but dare I confess that such total immersion in Christmas makes me sick of the sight of the shop for a little while. So on Christmas Eve, I shut up shop till New Year, and jump in the car and escape."

I waited for him to tell me his destination, sure it would be somewhere exciting. I hoped he might invite me too. The Scottish Highlands, perhaps, or an isolated cottage on the Cornish coast? Maybe the opposite extreme – a balmy tropical island where Christmas lunch would be exotic fruits and local rum punch. Not that he could get there by car. Perhaps he just meant driving to the airport.

Or – surely not – Australia for roast turkey on the beach with Celeste and their child? For a moment, I couldn't breathe.

"It keeps my parents happy, anyway." Ah, tropic of Clevedon, then. "After all, Christmas is all about family, isn't it?" Maybe Celeste came to them. "No matter how old your kids are, you want them around. I'm guessing you'll be off to your folks in Inverness?"

That burst my bubble. My personal festive vision morphed from opening romantic Christmas gifts on the shag-pile carpet in front of Hector's wood-burner to post-lunch Scrabble with my folks.

"Have you booked your flight yet?" he asked. "You'll need to apply early to get a decent price."

Now he couldn't wait to be rid of me.

"No, I'd better get on with it."

There didn't seem much else I could say without sounding offended or needy. I made an excuse to turn away from him so he couldn't spot the disappointment on my face.

"I'll make us a pot of tea in a minute, but first I'll need to get more teabags from the shop. I'll get my coat."

As I slipped out of the door to the High Street, Hector started to suspend plastic icicles in the window, like a latter-day Snow Queen.

16 The Christmas Kitchen

Having spent the morning festifying Hector's House, I thought the village shop looked awfully dull. When I arrived, Carol was sorting potatoes by size into three piles on the counter.

I fetched a box of teabags and held it up for her to see the price label. I couldn't help thinking there was more to her dislike of Christmas than the unhappy ending of her ill-fated romance half her lifetime ago, and I decided to do some gentle investigating.

"So does your birthday fall on Christmas Day? Is that why you're called Carol?" I asked innocently.

"Bless you, no, Sophie, though I am a Capri Sun." As she reached for the accounts book to log my purchase against Hector's account, the door jangled to admit the man in the white coat who had been delivering cakes the previous week.

"Down there on the right, please," said Carol, pointing listlessly. "And remember you said you'd replace unsold stock with fresh cakes for free."

I stood back to let him pass.

"Actually, my birthday's on Twelfth Night," said Carol, turning back to me. She'd meant Capricorn. "Not that it's much cause for celebration when you reach my age. No more than Christmas, really. Though I suppose it means I get a day off for once."

"So what do you do on Christmas Day?" I wondered whether she had relatives in the village.

"Once I've shut the shop on Christmas Eve, I'm on my own," she said, categorising the last of the potatoes and wiping her hands on her apron.

"But I expect you go away to relatives?" I assumed she must have some family members somewhere, even if not in the village. "I'm off to Inverness to stay with my parents."

She shook her head sadly. "No, I've no family left. I can't spend it with my parents or my husband or my children. So I do the obvious thing."

That sounded ominous. I wondered what she was going to say next. Cry? Get drunk? Take sleeping pills and hibernate till it was all over?

"I go and help the homeless, of course. Not that we have any in Wendlebury, but there's a place down in Slate Green where they cook Christmas dinner for anyone who's hard up or lonely. People who use the foodbank can come, and anyone living in hostels or on their own. We serve dozens of dinners and give everyone a present and a card. I knit plenty of hats, gloves and scarves each autumn and wrap them up specially."

This was the obvious thing only for someone as kind-hearted as Carol. I felt churlish now for sulking about Hector's plans. Goodness, I was lucky.

Carol pulled out from beneath the counter a collection box labelled Slate Green Christmas Kitchen Appeal, the first sign of the festive season in the shop. I reached in my pocket for some loose change and dropped it in the slot.

"Thank you, Sophie. And you can be the first to sign the cards."

She produced two large Christmas cards, one addressed "To our friends at Slate Green Christmas Kitchen" and the other "To the Wendlebury Barrow Community".

"This one's for the guests to show them we're thinking of them on Christmas Day, and the other's a paper-saving tradition for the village. Instead of everyone sending each other a Christmas card, we all sign this one, and the names get printed in the January parish magazine."

She leaned forward confidentially.

"The list is always worth reading because it brings you up to date with everyone's status."

I could imagine her checking it to see whether any men were newly single.

"People use it to announce changes, such as when a couple gets engaged, or a partner moves in, or when they're expecting a baby in the new year. 'From Janet and John plus bump', that sort of thing. Also, you can tell when people's dogs have died or they've got new ones."

I extracted a pen from my handbag.

"Their dogs sign the cards too?"

"Well, the owners sign for them. One Christmas we were all convinced that this couple who usually kept themselves to themselves had had twins, because her husband had signed for the two of them plus Sharon and Tracy. It turned out those were their new puppies. We worked it out eventually, but only after I'd knitted her two baby blankets. Fortunately she assumed they were for the dogs."

"What lucky puppies," I said, glad Carol hadn't been embarrassed. I wondered how many garments she'd knitted over the years for other people's babies, wishing she had some of her own.

"Still, that wasn't as unfortunate as when we all thought Mr Brown was announcing a sex-change operation. It looked like he'd signed it as Alexa instead of Alex, so what else was I to think?"

I shook my head sympathetically, trying not to smile.

"Turned out it was just young Tommy Crowe up to his tricks, adding extras to the card when I wasn't looking. I had wondered how I'd managed to miss Prince Charles. And Father Christmas."

The baker laughed aloud, making us realise he'd been eavesdropping as he restocked the cake shelf. That made me regret telling Carol that I was going away over Christmas. Now he knew my house would be empty.

We watched him carry his tray of stale cakes back to his van. The tray was nearly as full as the one he'd delivered. As he returned to give Carol his bill, I bade them both goodbye and headed back to Hector's House. The baker's unmarked white van was easy to identify by the stray mince pie wicking up rain in a puddle behind its back doors. There's nothing to this detection lark once you get attuned to it.

17 Christmas Past

"I wouldn't mind one of these myself," I said.

Hector smiled kindly. "You're never too old for an Advent calendar." He pulled one off the top of the pile and slipped it into my handbag.

In the stockroom after the shop had closed, we'd just unpacked the box of Advent calendars that were to be the children's gifts from our visiting Santa. Hector had ordered a traditional design showing a stable scene beneath a glittery giant star, deeming it a universally acceptable classic. Sticking with a single style also meant that we could give the same thing to all the children, regardless of age or gender. Any left over could be returned to the shop stock for sale in the normal way.

Unfortunately, the manufacturers packaged the calendars in cheap-looking plastic wrappers, so we were adding value and class by repackaging them. Hector took the calendars out of their plastic bags, slipped them into stiff bright green envelopes, added a festive sticker on the front, and passed them to me. My job was to seal each flap with traditional red sealing wax. We were quite the production line.

Working together cosily like this provided the perfect opportunity for some idle festive chat, with no customers around to listen in.

"So who was this bloke that turned Carol against Christmas?" I asked Hector.

He peeled a cheery reindeer from the sticker sheet, stuck it on the front of his current envelope and set it down on the table, halting our production line to consider.

"Sophie, the thing is, I'd love to tell you, but there are some things I just can't share."

I slumped back in my chair, setting down the sealing wax on its saucer to catch the drips.

"Was he already married? Was that the problem?"

Hector, tight-lipped, shook his head.

"Can't you just tell me a little bit, so that I don't jump to the wrong conclusion?"

Hector passed me his latest envelope.

"You? As if!"

I raised my eyebrows. "Go on, you can tell me. What happened? Did you see her kissing Santa Claus?"

He laughed. "No, not Santa Claus." Then his face went more serious. "No, it was someone much less fun. Although he did come for her in the dead of night to whisk her away while the village slept."

Hector slit the next plastic package, slid out the calendar, and dropped the cellophane in the bin.

I frowned. "Why the need for such secrecy?"

He picked up another envelope.

"Her beau was so unsuitable that there's no way her parents would have given the match their blessing. And they would have been right."

I sighed. "Poor Carol. She has such rotten taste in men."

Hector pointed his scissors at me accusingly. "She did used to fancy me, you know."

I grinned. "I rest my case."

He sealed the envelope, added a sticker, and passed it across to me.

"He was even more unsuitable than me, if you can believe that."

I held the stick of sealing wax over the candle flame.

"Not Billy, surely?"

He glanced up at me uncertainly.

"No, not Billy. Even worse than Billy."

I flipped over the envelope and dropped a few blobs over the flap, pressing the little metal seal with a heart motif firmly down into the scarlet wax.

"I can't think of anyone less eligible in the village than Billy."

"You'd be surprised," said Hector, sticking a holly wreath down. "In any case, as I said at the outset, you wouldn't know him anyway."

I picked up my newly sealed envelope and blew on the wax to harden it.

"It seems strange to think of her running away. I always assumed she'd been here for ever, always in the village shop."

Hector raised his eyebrows. "Our customers might think the same about me. But there's no reason to."

"But surely her parents didn't expect that she'd stay with them for ever? She had to have a life and a home of her own."

He passed me the next envelope. "Yes, just not with the reprobate she chose."

I picked up the sealing wax stick again.

"And they didn't even have a home to go to. The chap just picked her up in his van and off they went. That was the last anyone heard from her for ages. No mobile phones in those days, of course, and far fewer security cameras."

I stared into the flame, watching the wax liquefy.

"Gosh, you make them sound like Bonnie and Clyde. They weren't, were they? They didn't go off and rob banks"

Hector laughed. "No, not quite. But I think he ended up in prison for assault – whether on her or someone else, I'm not entirely sure. Remember, I was just a kid when all this happened, so I'm sure my mum spared me some of the details when she told me about it. Anyway, I gather Carol had a bad time till she returned the following Christmas Eve."

"And her parents took her back in?"

Hector nodded. "The Prodigal Daughter. They killed the fatted calf. Well, the fatted turkey, anyway."

I dripped the wax on to the next envelope.

"Did he ever come back to find her?"

Hector scrunched up another plastic wrapper. "Nope."

"Even though he was from the village?"

I fixed Hector with a steely look, determined to identify the jilting Clyde. I might not be able to wreak vengeance on Carol's behalf, but at least if I knew who he was, I couldn't accidentally be nice to him.

Suddenly I cried out in pain as the liquefied wax ran down my fingers and congealed in my palm. "Ouch! Oh, ouch! Why is this so much hotter than candle wax? It's like molten lava. I've got a volcano in my hand!"

I waved my hand aloft, pain searing up my arm. Hector scraped back his chair and rushed round to my side of the table.

"Quick, run it under the cold tap, for at least ten minutes, until it stops burning."

He steered me out of the stockroom and into the tearoom and turned on the tap. By this time, I was crying with pain.

"Hector, how did you ever think this was a good idea?" I sobbed, as the freezing water darkened my cuffs. "Why couldn't we just lick the flaps?"

18 Logging On

"Sophie, I need to borrow your laptop tomorrow."

Not wanting to have an argument about it on my doorstep, I beckoned Damian into my cottage. Nor did I want to lose the heat from my front room, having just spent half an hour struggling to light the wood-burner.

He perched on the edge of the armchair by the fire. I was glad this didn't appear to be a lingering social call.

"What do you want it for?"

Damian waved a hand dismissively at my perfectly reasonable question.

"Oh, just stuff."

Alarm bells started ringing in my head. "Damian, my laptop is my workhorse. I write on it, and I use it for my teaching records for the children I help with their reading after school. It's indispensable. If you download anything on it that shouldn't be seen by primary school children—"

"Oh, for goodness' sake, Sophie, why do you always think the worst of me?"

I said nothing.

"Anyway, you won't be using it during the school day, not till your precious after-school pupils arrive. I'll give it back to you by home-time."

Detecting the scent of scorching denim, he pulled his legs back from the fire, now blazing noisily out of control.

He donned the oven glove from the hearth and knelt down by the side of the wood-burner.

"You're meant to flip the knob at the back and close the holes at the front once you've got it going, you know." He reached his gloved hand round to do just that.

The flames immediately subsided into a comforting, steady flicker, and I stopped worrying so much about how long it might take the fire brigade in Slate Green to reach Wendlebury.

"How did you know how to do that?" I asked.

Damian's previous grasp of domestic heating had excluded knowing how and when to turn the 'on' switch to 'off'.

"Carol taught me. She's got a wood-burner in her sitting room, and it's glorious. We're very cosy in the evenings."

Not too cosy, I hoped.

"So how is it going with Carol?"

Damian smiled distantly. "Fine. She's a very good cook."

I tried not to take that as a veiled insult to my skills in the kitchen.

"Talks a lot, though."

I hoped he was doing her the courtesy of listening.

"I expect she's glad to have a conversation that lasts longer than it takes for someone to do their shopping. She's been living alone for years since her parents died. She must miss them."

"She certainly talks a lot about them. Sometimes it feels like they've never left."

He looked about for a moment, taking in May's many souvenirs of her foreign travels, still dotted about the place. I wondered how long I'd need to live here before my possessions outnumbered hers.

"She's never been married, you know," said Damian suddenly. "You'd think a woman like her would have wanted to get married."

I sighed. "Just wanting doesn't make it possible. She's never had the chance. The same goes for babies. She's the sort who'd be uncomfortable having babies without being married, so she's missed out on both counts."

Damian seemed unconvinced.

"You have to understand that she chose to spend her prime looking after her invalid mother, in a village where it's nigh impossible to meet eligible men."

He shot me a reproachful look. "You seem to have wasted no time in finding one."

We both fell silent for a few minutes, gazing at the fire.

"Carol told me she used to be in love with your Hector," he said eventually. "And the last vicar."

I pursed my lips. "I wouldn't call it love. Those were both just crushes, really. Poor Carol always goes for the wrong kind of man. The vicar was awful."

I expected him to make a cutting remark about Hector, but the warmth of the fire was making us too lazy to squabble. Besides, it was nearly Christmas.

"Shall I put another log on for you?" Damian asked, to my surprise.

He flipped the knob at the back again, then clanked open the little black doors. The fire immediately burned brighter for the influx of oxygen. He selected a chunky log from the dwindling stack in the inglenook and placed it carefully on top of the embers.

"You see, it's just at the right stage to add more wood now. Do you want me to bring more logs in for you? I assume you've got some in a shed at the back."

My instinct was to say, "No thank you, I'm perfectly capable of doing it myself," then I realised the benefits of his offer. I could stay snug by the fire, keep my hands clean, and avoid any wildlife lurking in the shadows of the woodshed.

"Thank you, Damian, that would be great." Maybe some of Carol's kindness was rubbing off on him.

While he busied himself in the garden, I picked up "A Christmas Carol" from my desk and read a few more pages. When he returned with a very full basket, he set it down carefully on the tiled hearth so as not to drop sawdust on the rug. Carol must have been housetraining him.

"Carol reckons log fires are good for building strong arm muscles." He grinned. "She said in winter her triceratops are always bigger than in summer."

"Triceps," I translated.

He resumed his perch on the armchair.

"Oh, by the way, I'll need to borrow your internet too."

I knew his generosity concealed an ulterior motive. "If you're getting along with Carol so famously, why can't you use hers? Or her computer, come to that?"

Damian gazed into the fire, which was ticking over nicely now. "Hers is ancient and slow. Besides, it would feel wrong, like rifling through her handbag."

More like he didn't want her to see what he was doing on it.

"And you don't mind delving in my handbag?"

He flashed me a flirtatious look. "Oh no, that's not the same thing at all. There's nothing in your handbag that I haven't seen before." I threw a cushion at his head. "So is that a yes, then?"

I gazed at the full log basket. I am too easily bought. "OK. I'll give you a spare key and you can let yourself in while I'm at work tomorrow." I switched to my dog-trainer voice. "But don't change any of the settings, and don't go on sites that cost money."

He leapt up from his chair, mission accomplished. "Thanks, Sophie, you're a pal. I'll be round about lunchtime, and I'll drop your laptop up to you at the bookshop as soon as I'm done with it, so that you've got it ready for your after-school coaching sessions."

"OK, but this is just the once, all right?" I didn't want these unsolicited evening calls to become a habit. At least, not while I had a full log basket.

I spent the rest of the evening password-protecting all the files on my laptop.

19 Keyed Up

I was glad Hector was in the stockroom when Damian came bounding into the shop the next afternoon, clutching my laptop.

"Thanks for everything, Sophie."

I put down the publisher's catalogue that I'd been browsing through.

"You're welcome. Did you get what you wanted?" I hoped my casual tone might fool him into inadvertently revealing exactly what that was. But he just nodded and looked smug.

"And don't worry, I didn't run your bill up or change your precious settings." He looked at his watch. "Right, I'd best get going, then. I usually take a cup of tea down to the shop for Carol about now."

I raised my eyebrows. "She'll miss you when you've gone."

I hoped he didn't take that to mean that I would miss him too. As he turned to go, he stopped in the doorway to say over his shoulder, "By the way, I've left a little surprise at your house as a thank you."

And with that he slammed the door too hard and was gone.

Silent as a ghost – well, not Marley's ghost, obviously – Hector emerged from the stockroom, looking irritated. I didn't want him to misconstrue our conversation.

"He's only been using my laptop."

"In your house?"

"He needed the wifi."

Hector pointed to the shop's free wifi code on the chalkboard by the door. "Why didn't he use Carol's? Or ours? Or the pub's?"

I wished I'd thought of that. "Oh. OK. I'll tell him for next time. But he was only using it while I was out."

"So he has a key to your cottage, does he? That's more than I've got."

"Only for today."

I thought it better not to tell him that I'd forgotten to ask for it back.

As I strode home after work, I couldn't help but wonder what Damian had been up to. Was his request to use my wifi just a ruse to gain access to my cottage while I was out? And what was the surprise he had in store for me?

I was mightily relieved not to find him naked on the hearth rug. Instead, the only evidence of his presence was a trail of muddy footprints to and from the kitchen.

My eye followed them to the inglenook, now stacked full of logs. Not only were there enough logs to spare me a couple of weeks of hauling them in from outside, the pile was also beautifully stacked, creating a pleasing mosaic effect of neatly aligned cross-sections of trees. On the rug just to one side, the log basket was filled with newly split kindling, taking care of my fire-lighting needs too. He must have taken ages.

I sank down on to the sofa in amazement, savouring the fresh scent. It was like inhaling a forest.

Touched by Damian's unexpected kindness, I almost forgave him the shower of biscuit crumbs that had settled on my keyboard like snow, and the fact that he'd deleted from the browsing history any record of what he'd used my laptop for.

Perhaps he hadn't used it at all, and the crumbs were a plant to make it look as if he had.

I wrote a note in biro on the back of my hand to ask him to return my key. But I had no time to ponder further. It was the Wendlebury Writers' night, and after a hasty supper eaten on the sofa, gazing at my new wooden art installation, I headed back up to Hector's House to open it for our meeting.

20 The Advent Anthology

"I wouldn't be surprised if they recruited some more members now they've got that gorgeous new director." Local dentist Jacky looked away, slightly abashed, as she spoke. I'd forgotten several of the Wendlebury Writers had left the Players after falling out with the previous director.

I sighed to myself. Why did people always see Damian's looks before his personality?

Karen's quick response spared me from answering. "If people join the Players for the wrong reasons, the quality of their show will be at risk. What they really need are some more male actors."

"I don't see what all the fuss is about," said Dinah briskly. I was glad to know that at least one of the Writers was immune to Damian's charms. "Women can always play men's parts. Anyway, enough about the Players. What about our own Christmas event?" Dinah tapped the first point on her short agenda. "Have you all finished your pieces for our afternoon of festive readings?"

We'd agreed at the previous week's meeting to write a festive story, essay or poem, no more than three minutes long, to read at one of Hector's Sunday openings. We each produced folded pieces of paper, as if presenting homework to a strict teacher. Dinah looked pleased. The event had been her idea, an addition to our usual start-of-term open mic night, and she'd already persuaded Hector that it might be an extra draw to customers during the Christmas shopping season.

"Come on. Let's hear what you've all come up with. A two-sentence summary. Your elevator pitch."

She looked to Karen, sitting to her left. Karen took her cue. "I've written a very short story, just five hundred words, about a woman stuck in a supermarket queue with a trolley full of fancy Christmas food that she can't afford. Realising she'd have a happier Christmas if she focused her time on her family instead of shopping and cooking, she abandons the trolley and goes straight home. The story closes with her family having fun over a board game and bacon sandwiches on Christmas Day. The message is that Christmas is about quality time with family, not reckless and unnecessary extravagance."

Dinah nodded approval. Timidly I ventured a suggestion. "Maybe to reflect the fact that we're holding it in a bookshop, you could have them sitting round the fire sharing a book instead of a board game? Maybe "A Christmas Carol"?"

Dinah shook her head. "Wouldn't chime with the theme. Remember Scrooge orders the biggest turkey in the shop."

"Yes, but not for himself. It's for the Cratchit family."

"They could send a goat to Oxfam," said Jessica.

"I'll work on it," said Karen quickly.

Next round the table was Jacky.

"I hope you'll forgive the shop talk, but I've written a story about a lonely bachelor dentist who volunteers to man the emergency service on Christmas Day. His only patient is a long-lost girlfriend who's just broken a tooth on a sixpence in a Christmas pudding. The theme is that love and luck aren't always where you look for them. It's also a useful warning not to hide hard things in soft food, but that's by the by."

Then came Jessica's turn. Knowing her speciality was animal poems, I almost suggested she write a comic verse about a dog in a manger, but didn't want to pay the customary 50p fine for clichés that the group imposed.

"My Christmas poem is about the nativity from the viewpoint of a lamb, which compares itself to the baby Jesus. It's called 'Innocents'."

"And they will both be slaughtered when they grow up. Perfect." That came from Dinah, of course.

Jessica flinched. She was vegetarian.

"Oh no, I haven't taken it that far. I just allude to the love between mother and child, and how a mother is the centre of the new-born's world at first. But I could add some ominous brooding on what lies ahead, if you think that would help."

Her fellow poet Bella got in quickly before Dinah could comment any further. "I've taken the weather as my subject and written about the absurdity of associating Christmas with snow, when there's never any snow in Bethlehem. Then I segue into a comparison between snowflakes and stars, which of course are inextricably linked with the Bible story."

Dinah nodded approvingly. "Interesting take."

Julia unfolded her sheet next. "Well, you won't be surprised to hear I've written something historical. I've described how Christmas has been celebrated through the ages, the Christian church subsuming pagan traditions along the way. I hope it won't sound too much like a history lesson. Though to be honest, I did draw on the material that I've often used in school for the last lesson before Christmas."

"No problem, as long as you haven't written it like a lecture," said Dinah. "Is it non-fiction? That's a change for you."

"No, I've presented it as the diary of someone who's lived a very long time and seen it all happen. A bit like Virginia Woolf's Orlando, Sophie, so you should like it."

I tried to look as if I knew who Orlando was.

Next it was Louisa's turn. She was a crime writer.

"I didn't want to write anything that might scare people at Christmas," she said. "So instead I've written about a long-term unemployed man who decides to shoplift Christmas presents because he can't afford to buy them. He disguises himself as Santa, on the basis that no-one would suspect Santa of theft, and thinks he's been rumbled when the store manager collars him. It turns out the store's real Santa has been suddenly taken ill, so they ask the man to stand in. He does it so well that they offer him a job, and to stay on after Christmas as store detective."

Dinah nodded.

"I suppose you can't have Christmas without crime, can you?" she said. "Which leads us on to you, Sophie."

I coughed nervously, not sure whether I was comfortable with her train of thought.

"Similar to my 'Travels with my Aunt's Garden' column, I've written about the poinsettia." Writing about plants was becoming my speciality, not because I knew anything about them, but because my aunt's eclectic garden inspired me. And it was an easy subject to research. "It's got a fascinating history with lots of different stories attached to it, mostly associating it with Christmas, but also with Easter in some places. We tend to think of the poinsettia as an American import, but actually it's quite cosmopolitan."

Sounds of approval issued from around the table.

"So that just leaves you, Dinah," I said, relieved to have got my turn over with.

Dinah sat up straight in her seat.

"I've done a feminist take on the notion of Santa Claus. My short story, 'The Multi-tasking Christmas', allocates the role of gift distribution to Mrs Claus instead. Setting her husband to shovelling snow to clear the path for the reindeer – an endless task at the North Pole – she reorganises his workshop and distribution system to make it much more efficient."

"Is it funny?" Bella asked hopefully. "I mean, it's not a political tract, is it?"

"It's lighthearted enough," said Dinah. "But if any men want to infer a hint to get their Christmas act together, that's fine by me."

There was a moment's silence while we all digested what we'd shared.

"Gosh, I think we're doing jolly well," declared Jessica. "That's a great mix of pieces, covering Christmas from lots of different angles without any overlap. I think it'll be a lovely event."

Even Dinah looked pleased. "More by luck than – er – careful advance planning."

"What a shame there's only one performance," said Karen, one of the former Players. "It'll all be over far too quickly."

Bella rapped the table for attention. "Why don't I type the pieces up and photocopy them?" She was a wiz on the computer, thanks to her work as parish clerk. "Then we could hand out hard copies."

"Or sell them," said Dinah. "Though I'm not sure people who are there to do Christmas shopping will want to spend money on photocopied sheets."

"If only it were in book form, it would make a lovely Christmas present," said Jacky. "I'd buy copies for my friends and family. My mum would love one."

Gazing at the shop counter, where Hector wrote his own books, I had a brilliant idea. "I know, I'll get Hector to make a proper printed book for us. That way we could sell it as a Christmas present, and we'd have a great souvenir of the day for ourselves."

Everyone fell upon the idea at once, clearly sharing my enthusiasm. Then Dinah held up her hand, as if spotting a problem. "Wait a minute, how does Hector know how to do that?"

I turned cold for a moment, realising how close I'd come to giving away Hector's secret identity as the romantic novelist Hermione Minty.

"Oh, you know Hector," I said brightly. "He's a dark horse. He knows how to do all sorts of things you wouldn't expect him to."

Dinah raised an eyebrow at me and opened her mouth to speak, but Jessica's enthusiastic interruption spared me from further probing. "Oh, do ask him, please, Sophie. It would be so exciting to have our own book out. I'd buy copies for all my friends and relations for Christmas."

"We could take a stall at the school Christmas fair, too," added Karen. "They'd make great stocking fillers."

Dinah hesitated for a moment. "Worst case, he says no. Although who buys books by unknown authors?"

"We're not unknown around here," said Bella, reasonably enough.

I spotted a chance to show off knowledge I'd gained from working at Hector's House.

"Lesser-known writers' books sell better if they have a cover endorsement by a famous name, usually an author or other celebrity."

"Then let's get one," said Jessica.

"Not a celebrity, please," said Dinah, making air quotes around 'celebrity'. "For our own credibility, it must be an author. Who's your current bestseller, Sophie?"

That was easy. I pointed to a stack of Hermione Minty books on the centre table.

"She'll do." Dinah minuted it like a done deal. "I'm putting you down to email a request to her publisher, Sophie. You'll have the most clout, as you're in the trade."

I forced a smile of assent.

"No problem, Dinah. Leave it with me."

We spent the rest of the meeting reading our pieces aloud to each other. I needed to fill my water glass twice during my turn. My mouth was as dry as a sandbox.

When Dinah called the meeting to a close, the Wendlebury Writers set off home, leaving me to shut up the shop. Just as I was setting the alarm, I heard Dinah's voice floating back through the chill night air.

"By the way, Sophie, when you're on to Hermione Minty, could you also invite her to be our guest of honour when we launch the book?"

Then there was a clunk above my head, and I looked up to see Hector peering down at me from his front room window.

21 Cocoa with Hermione

"What was that about Hermione Minty?"

In the darkness, I couldn't tell whether he was pleased or cross.

"Do you want to come up and tell me about it?"

I didn't, actually. I glanced at my watch, thinking to cry off on the grounds of the late hour, but it was only just gone nine.

"I'll come down and let you in."

Without waiting for an answer, he withdrew his head and closed the window.

A few minutes later I was curled up in my usual fireside chair, sipping a very dark cocoa, hesitantly unveiling the Writers' plan to self-publish an anthology. Well, to get Hector to publish it for us, anyway. Convincing him was proving harder than I'd expected. He had a string of objections.

"For one thing, you're about six months too late. Christmas books are usually launched in September, to give the reps a chance to pitch them to bookshops."

Embarrassed by my rookie error, I thought fast. "Yes, but we don't have any reps to pitch for us, and the only bookseller we want to sell it for us is you. Consider this my pitch."

His ensuing silence gave me the courage to strengthen my case.

"Besides, you'd already agreed with Dinah that we could hold our festive reading event in Hector's House. And the Writers are kindly giving up their Sunday afternoon to come and support your shop, and advertising it to all their friends and relations. For free."

I gave him a hard stare, and he seemed to waver, so I steamrollered on.

"You're always telling me that having visiting writers in the shop for book signings attracts more customers. Well, you've got the Writers. Now all we need is the book."

Was I laying it on too thick? Hector kept me waiting, shrewd enough to use the power of silence in negotiating, a tactic I knew about but never managed to employ. He leaned forward, added another couple of logs to the wood-burner, and sat back, hands clasped thoughtfully on his lap.

Finally he deigned to speak. "OK, but only because it's you, and strictly as a one-off. It'll take me a good few hours to format your manuscript on the computer and upload it to the print-on-demand service I use, and you'll have to make do with one of their stock covers. And I'll only sell it if you get it professionally proofread. I can probably get Hermione's proofreader to squeeze it into her busy schedule as it'll be a very short book. I'll deduct her cost out of the profits."

I nodded dumbly. At this point, if he'd stipulated we should sign the books in our own blood, I'd have agreed.

"The shop will take its usual cut for every book sold. Normal business rates, mind. And I'll expect the Writers each to do a bit of Christmas shopping while they're here."

He finished his cocoa like a man who had earned it, and set the empty mug on the hearth.

"Thank you so much, Hector," I said in a small voice. "I'm sure the Writers will agree."

Hector relaxed for a moment, then his brow furrowed. "One question, though. How did you explain away that I knew how to self-publish books? I hope you didn't give away my alter ego?"

I smiled innocently.

"They're ready to believe you can do anything."

Hector grinned.

"Just one of my many superpowers, I suppose." He wagged a reproachful finger at me. "Never underestimate a bookseller."

A shower of sparks fizzed against the wood-burner's glass door, reminding me of Fireworks Night. Sipping cocoa, cosy and warm in the best company that I could think of, I believed all was right with the world – until I remembered the Writers' final request.

I rattled it out quickly before I lost my nerve. "Oh, and they'd also like a cover endorsement from a well-known author to add credibility and appeal. Like Hermione Minty." I leaned forward, my hands on his knees, eyes as wide and appealing as I could make them without looking deranged.

Hector put his hands over his face and sighed. "I suppose I could ask her. But only if she likes what they've written. She has her principles."

"And I'll recommend they all buy one of Hermione's books to show their appreciation."

"As long as they don't expect her to come in and sign them."

He set his empty mug on the hearth.

"Signed copies?" I sat up straight. "What a brilliant idea!"

"What? Are you mad?"

"But you told me before that you sell them at a premium on eBay."

"Yes, but that's remote, altogether different from flaunting my secret identify on my doorstep."

I waved my hand dismissively. "It's not as if she has to sign them in front of everybody."

"Ha! I should think not, indeed!"

"No, you just do it in private before you put them out on display. No-one need ever know. Just think, it would give you a Christmas exclusive that no other bookshop could offer."

Hector fetched the brandy bottle and balloon glasses from the cabinet, and set them down on the hearth.

"I'd better top up my superpowers," he said, unscrewing the lid and splashing a generous amount in each glass.

"Don't worry, Hector," I said, taking one of them from him. "Hermione's secrets are safe with me."

22 Adding Depth

Damian punctuated his opening address to the cast with the critical facial expressions and gestures of an Oscar-winning director. He hadn't become an actor for nothing. Then, to my surprise and delight, he began to play his part genuinely, coaching the cast to get the best out of their lines and choreographing effective moves to freshen up the familiar story.

As I sat at the back of the hall, under instructions to shout whenever anyone wasn't projecting their voice, I mused on how modern day wise men might undertake their journey. They'd probably fly business class, while the holy family caught an overcrowded bus. Perhaps Mary and Joseph's subsequent flight into Egypt would have been a literal one – via a no-frills airline, of course. What a worry if it got delayed or cancelled. Would it be possible to smuggle a baby through passport control to escape the slaughter ordered by King Herod? And would they get the gold, frankincense and myrrh past security? They'd probably have to put it in the hold, not their in-flight bags. That would make a big dent in their baggage allowance.

"Sophie? Are you awake back there?"

I jumped. "Sorry, Damian."

He paced backwards towards me, never taking his eye off the stage. "I'm not surprised you drifted off. It's all too flat, too static. We need to make it more three-dimensional."

"What, give the audience 3D glasses?"

"No, stupid. We're going to have to bring the actors out into the auditorium. The audience needs to feel involved. They should feel as if they're travelling on the donkey with Mary and Joseph, stowaways on the wise men's camels, apprentices accompanying the shepherds."

"Intern to a wise man – that would be a dream job."

"What?" Damian gave me a withering look.

"Do you mean audience participation? I hope we're not in danger of veering into panto. 'Where's the star?' 'It's behind you!'"

"Of course not," he said crossly. "I mean, let's take the action off the stage and bring it down into the auditorium. We'll have the journeys going up and down the aisle and around the perimeter of the hall to give some idea of the arduous nature of the trip and the distance involved."

He looked around the hall for inspiration. "This is a crap setting. It's hard to create an atmosphere of awe and wonder surrounded by posters for barn dances and ballet lessons, and paintings of clowns by playgroup children."

He really didn't have a clue about village life.

"You have to remember, Damian, this isn't a dedicated theatre. It's a resource shared by the whole community. It's used by everybody for everything, from children's birthday parties and old people's bingo to five-a-side football and WI."

"Then we need somewhere that doesn't have all those unhelpful associations. Somewhere the audience can focus on the spell we'll be weaving about them."

"What about using the church?" I said, before I was even aware I'd thought of the idea. "Just being there will put people into an appropriate frame of mind before the play even begins."

Damian looked thoughtful. "I haven't been in there yet, but having seen it from the outside, I'd guess the scale and style of the architecture will offer us much greater scope than this tatty old shed."

I ignored that unmerited sideswipe, hoping no-one else had heard it. Damian had excellent projection.

"We'll have to ask the Reverend Murray when he arrives, of course," I said, glad to be flaunting my authority for a change. "But I expect Kate will be able to OK it in the meantime, as chair of the Parochial Church Council."

Damian looked sceptical. "I can't see any vicar objecting to a full house. Or to getting youngsters into church."

"And we'll have God on our side," I added cheerfully. "Which will probably cancel out the bad luck brought by children and animals."

Damian turned his back on me and headed back to the stage.

23 Saint Katherine

"Have you got Kate's phone number, please, Hector? I want to ask her permission to stage the nativity play in the church this year."

"That's rather coals to Newcastle, isn't it?" Hector pulled his mobile phone out of his front pocket and swiped through his contacts. He scribbled her number on the back of a discarded till receipt and passed it across.

"Precisely. That's why we want to stage it there. In its natural habitat."

I picked up the shop phone and punched in the number. Kate answered so quickly she made me jump.

"How about that for lightning reactions?" she said brightly. "I'm at my desk drowning in six months' paperwork. Please tell me you've called to distract me."

I laughed. "I certainly have. I wanted to ask you whether we might stage our nativity play at St Bride's, rather than the Village Hall. Damian and I thought it would offer more scope and be more effective. The Players thought when Mr Murray arrives, he wouldn't mind, but I wanted to ask you officially in his absence."

Kate sounded puzzled. "Damian? Who's Damian? I don't think I know a Damian in the village."

"He's my ex-boyfriend and a professional theatre director. He's come to guest-direct my nativity play."

Kate went quiet for a moment. "I take it you're at work just now?"

"Yes."

"Can I come down to talk to you about it over coffee?"

"Sure. Though I might have to break off if the shop gets busy."

"OK, I'll see you shortly."

I returned the handset to its cradle. Hector looked up expectantly.

"She's on her way."

"I'll take cover," he replied, heading to the stockroom.

"So tell me more about Damian. Is he Rex's successor?" Kate put her hands around her coffee cup to warm them after her chilly walk to the shop. "As director of the Players, I mean."

"Yes, but just for this one play. He's filling time between professional bookings in Europe."

She took a sip of coffee thoughtfully. "What does he look like? Have I met him?"

I hesitated to describe him, conscious that Hector might hear me.

"You might have seen him at the pub last week when you and Hector were having dinner there. He was playing darts with Ian's team."

Kate perked up. "Ooh, yes, I remember. Tall, muscular Viking type. Strong blond good looks."

I tried to sound unconvinced to avoid hurting Hector's feelings. "If you say so."

"And why does he want to use the church instead of the School Hall or Village Hall?"

"He wants awe and wonder. The hall's a bit thin on those. The church is much bigger too. We'd like to use

108

the whole church, to give a sense of the distance travelled."

Kate nodded. "Plus of course it would make great use of the parallel between man's spiritual journey from font to altar and Christ's journey from manger to cross."

Just as I was starting to feel out of my depth, who should walk in but Damian? He strode straight over to our table.

"Here's your spare door key."

He leaned over, pulled open the top pocket of my shirt, and dropped the key inside. I clapped my hand to my chest to cover it, embarrassed by his over-familiar gesture. He flashed a smile at the startled Kate.

"I realised when I got back to Carol's that I already had a spare key anyway, so that made two. I thought you'd want the spare-spare back in case you want to give it to someone else."

I hoped that didn't make me sound fast and loose.

Kate looked from me to him and back again. "You're not staying at Sophie's, then?"

"Not at the moment." Damian beat me to replying. "I'm lodging with Carol while I help her fix up her house a bit."

Before I could deny his implication that he might move in with me in the future, an elderly couple entered the shop and came to stand pointedly at the counter, waiting to be served. I glanced at the stockroom door, willing Hector to emerge, but he stayed put.

"Excuse me, Kate."

As I got up to do my duty, Damian took my seat, and I left the two of them chatting while I dealt with the customers. Their complex order demanded too much of my concentration to allow me to listen in on Kate and Damian's conversation.

Just as I finished serving, Damian got up to leave, patting me on the head as he passed the counter. At the sound of the shop door closing, Hector came out of the stockroom and sat down by Kate. Kate almost immediately got up to leave and headed out of the door. This was starting to feel like a game of musical chairs. I wondered whether she was following Damian to check he wasn't really returning to my house.

Despatching my customers with a substantial haul of books, I looked across to Hector, expecting him to be pleased with the high value of my sale. Instead he was glowering at me.

"Kate told me to give you this message: 'Yes, that's fine, as long as he doesn't go raping and pillaging.' I take it that means something to you?"

I bit my lip.

"It means Damian can use the church to stage the nativity play, provided I keep him under control."

"And can you?"

I didn't answer.

24 Extras

As Mrs Broom sat down on a chair at the side of the school hall, I felt the pressure of 200 eyes turned upon me. Well, 199 actually, because one small boy in the youngest class was sporting a corrective patch beneath his glasses. I spotted Jemima, one of the children I was giving extra English lessons to in the shop after school. She gave me a proud wave from halfway back in the hall, digging her neighbour in the ribs to claim me as her friend. To bring me luck this morning, I'd slipped on to my wrist the string friendship bracelet she'd made me.

I took a deep breath and put on my teacher's voice.

"Well, children, I'm very pleased to see you all today. Damian and I have come to invite you to take part in a new kind of school Christmas play. Actually, it's a very old kind of play – a traditional nativity play about the birth of Jesus. This year, you're going to have an exciting opportunity to perform it in the church at Christmas. And it won't just be you. Your teachers will be acting in it too."

A ripple of chatter ran through the room, with many children darting excited glances at the teachers.

"The village drama group, the Wendlebury Players, will also be in it, and Damian, who is a professional theatre director, will be in charge. I've written it especially for you, so it will be a world premiere, which means it will be the first time it's been performed anywhere in the world."

A boy towards the back of the hall, where the older children sat, put up his hand. "Is this instead of a pantomime, miss, or as well as?"

"Instead of. We thought it was time for a change and a new challenge for you."

"Oh no, it isn't," heckled a wag from the top class.

"Oh yes, it is!" cried another.

I held my hand up for silence, as Mrs Broom had done during the Remembrance Day assembly, and found it surprisingly effective.

"Now, before I pass you over to Damian, who will tell you about the rehearsals, does anyone have any questions?"

I panned the room.

A girl of about seven put her hand up.

"Will we be doing Nativity 1, 2 or 3?"

I cast a pleading look to Damian, who shrugged. I hadn't heard of any sequels.

Mrs Broom came to our rescue. "Miss Sayers has been living abroad for the last few years, children, so she won't have seen that popular series of family films about schools doing nativity plays. Which is probably just as well."

The teachers chuckled behind their hands.

"Yes, but will we be doing the one with Martin Clunes?" persisted the little girl. "That's my favourite."

"Will Martin Clunes be in it?" said the girl next to her. "My mum loves Martin Clunes."

"No, children, you will be the stars of this show. You and your teachers and the Wendlebury Players. Any sensible questions, please?"

I pointed to a little boy at the front who was waving his hand urgently. "Can I go to the toilet, please?" His teacher reached across to haul him up by the hand and send him off in the right direction.

"Will there be dancing?" This was from a dainty little girl of about nine who looked like the type to be into her ballet.

I glanced at Damian for help. He gave a slight nod.

"There might be."

"And songs with actions?" queried a little boy. "We like songs with actions."

"And tinsel," said another. "We always have lots of tinsel in our Christmas play. And balloons."

I signalled again for silence as other children called out increasingly outlandish suggestions. "Carol will be doing the costumes, and I know how much you love her Halloween outfits. So I think you can trust her to make you all look fantastic, with or without balloons. Now, Damian will tell you how it's going to work."

Damian turned to me to acknowledge my introduction courteously. I was beginning to feel like a television presenter on a chat show. We could have done with a curvy couch in a garish colour.

"OK, guys, here's the thing." It was immediately clear that he wasn't a teacher, which made me feel more confident in my own authority. "If you want to take part, you'll need to come to the Village Hall to rehearse from two till four every Saturday between now and the end of term, except for the dress rehearsal which will be in the church." He scanned the audience for a moment to check they'd absorbed what he'd been saying.

At the back of the hall, a tall girl put her hand up, tossing her long blonde hair.

"Please may I be Mary?"

A dozen more hands immediately shot up with the eagerness of the first volunteer. Damian ignored them, fixing the would-be Mary with his most winning gaze.

"The adults will be taking the speaking parts in the play, but I can see you would make the perfect angel."

The little girl's cheeks went rose-pink, and I wondered how many other girls would hatch a crush on Damian during his talk.

A small boy towards the front waved at Damian.

"Can I be Baby Jesus?"

The older children laughed, and Damian gave him a conspiratorial smile, as if the boy was playing for laughs. I didn't think he had been. "Well spotted that Jesus won't have a speaking part. But I think you'd be a bit big to play a baby, don't you?"

A murmur of agreement flickered across the room. "No, you'll be a terrific baby lamb, and everyone will think you're adorable."

Sensing a vacancy in the manger department, the children were quickly forthcoming with a flurry of other suggestions.

"You can have my baby sister."

"My cat Dinky would be just the right size."

"I've trained my puppy to lie down. You could use him."

"Have you seen my pony?"

"Can I be a gorilla?"

As the children's imaginations went into overdrive, Mrs Broom stood up, both arms raised, to call them to order.

"Now, children, let's give Miss Sayers and Mr – er – Drammaticas a big thank you for coming to tell us about this exciting new project, and for inviting you all to be a part of it. I'm sure we're all going to have a wonderful time. Your teachers will give you a note to take home for your families, so make sure you give it to them. It's important to attend as many rehearsals as you can, to make the play run smoothly."

For the first time, I realised that with just three Saturdays before the performance, we had only six hours to turn this willing but unpredictable horde into a coordinated cast. But at least I didn't have to worry about them learning lines.

As Damian and I crossed the playground on our way out, the school's morning break was just beginning, and children were charging about, full of energy, in the thin November sunshine. A girl of about seven came running across to tug at Damian's sleeve, egged on by a gaggle of her friends.

"Sir, my friend Milly loves you!" She ran off, giggling.

Nearby, a boy from the top class called out after her, "She won't get very far. Can't you see he loves her already?" He jabbed his thumb unmistakeably at me.

Damian laughed a little too quickly to be natural, and together we hurried towards the gate.

25 Teachers Join In

"To be honest, I'm glad I don't have many lines to learn, Sophie."

The reception class teacher took me into her confidence before we started blocking out the moves at the first full adult rehearsal. "It would be too embarrassing if I forgot them in front of the children."

Ian looked surprised. "I've always thought teachers were natural actors, standing in front of their class all day."

"Yes, but it's not as if we have to learn what we're going to say off by heart for every lesson in advance." She looked horrified at the thought. "Goodness knows, we've got enough lesson preparation to do without that."

Ian refused to be deterred. "But it must help to be able to stand up in front of a roomful of potentially critical kids every day, knowing you've got to perform, whatever happens."

She wrinkled her nose. "I suppose so. But teaching's mostly a one-woman show."

"Or one man," put in the Year 6 teacher. "I'm not a drag act."

"And this play's an ensemble piece," said the reception teacher.

"And it's featuring children and animals," added the Year 2 teacher.

117

"Children who are playing animals," I said quickly. "That's not the same thing at all. We've only got one real live animal – Janet, the donkey."

"Is that better or worse?" she replied. I hoped it would be better.

While the rest of the cast had a quick read-through of their lines, Carol and I set out chairs to mark key features of the church to which we'd only have access for the dress rehearsal. Carol was much more familiar with the layout of the church than I was.

"I expect you're looking forward to welcoming the Reverend Murray back again," I said to her as we set up two long rows to delineate the central aisle. "He seems to have been much loved."

"Yes, and his wife." Carol's smile didn't reach her eyes. I knew she must have been hoping for an unmarried vicar to fill the vacancy. Hector had once told me that it's a truth universally acknowledged that a single vicar must be in want of a wife.

"Take heart, Carol. You know he's only a stop-gap till they find a permanent replacement."

She gave a resigned smile. "Lately it does seem that vicars are like buses in this parish. You wait ages for one, then two come at once." The last one had only stayed a few weeks before circumstances despatched him elsewhere. "Otherwise in this parish, it feels like we've got no bus service at all, once you're too old to use the school bus."

I had no answer to that.

After the read-through, Damian ordered everyone to take their starting places. In our new venue, we wouldn't have a stage with wings, so everyone would have to be concealed about the set from the start, ready to make their entrance.

We made good progress, and the three kings were just processing up the aisle to join the stable scene when the hall door swung open and crashed closed. Damian, busy giving directions to the kings on how to deport themselves on arrival at their destination, ignored the interruption, but I looked round to see Tommy Crowe, wielding a battered video camera. He sidled up to me, agog to see his former primary school teachers kneeling before the village lollipop man and the lady from the pet shop.

"What on earth are they playing at?" Tommy could have taught the teachers a thing or two about voice projection. I shushed him.

"We're rehearsing for the nativity play, Tommy. That's the stable scene."

He glanced briefly at the stable, then turned round to survey the hall.

"You've made a right mess with all these chairs. You'd better clear those away when you've finished or you'll be in big trouble with the Hall Committee."

He started to dismantle the chairs representing the font, stacking them noisily.

"Tommy, no!" I hissed. "I know you're only trying to be helpful, but we need those there for now. They're showing us where to go. We're pretending we're in the church."

He looked dubiously at the chairs. "Well, if you say so, miss."

I could see he was restless and would benefit from being given something constructive to do, but asking Tommy for help was not without risks. I wondered what I could safely ask him to do, then glanced at the camera in his hand.

"Perhaps you'd like to film the rehearsal, then you could show it to Damian and the cast afterwards so they can see the play from where the audience would be sitting. I think that would be ever so helpful."

Gratified that I'd noticed his new toy and found a constructive use for it, Tommy immediately set to work. I sat in the font, or rather one of the chairs representing the font, and settled down to watch the rehearsal.

"So far, so good," I said to Damian in a congratulatory tone. "Now all we need to do is weave in a hundred children, and we're there."

Tommy bounded up to show Damian his recording. "I've been your cameraman. Miss told me it would help you."

To my relief, Damian seemed receptive. "Let's see it, then."

Leaving the rest of us to tidy away the tables and chairs, Damian stood watching Tommy's replay, and by the time they were done, everyone else but me had gone home.

"Very helpful, Tommy, thank you," Damian was saying as I rejoined them. I was glad Damian was being kind to Tommy. We didn't want to alienate Tommy, with his reputation for pranks. "Can you come and do the same on Saturday at two o'clock for the children's rehearsal?"

Tommy couldn't have looked more pleased if he'd been offered a Hollywood contract. "Yeah, sure, if you like."

I was pleased too. "That's great, Tommy. Could you bring it over to Hector's House to show me afterwards?

I'll have to work Saturday afternoon, so I won't be able to watch it live."

"You leave it to me, miss," said Tommy. "You can count on me."

26 All Quiet

"Do you think it's the American influence?"

The previous Thursday had been Thanksgiving in the USA, followed by Black Friday, when people start Christmas shopping with their last pay packets before the Christmas holiday. I hadn't expected it to trigger a rush on the shops in sleepy Wendlebury.

"I don't think so. I don't think it's even the British influence. It's more likely something else is happening in the village this afternoon that's squeezing all our business into the morning. A sudden rush of children like this is usually a clue to an imminent birthday party."

I clapped my hand to my forehead. "Of course! The children's nativity play rehearsal starts in ten minutes, so they're all on their way there."

Jemima came up to the counter and handed me a slim pink paperback and ten fifty-pence coins. "I've been saving my pocket money."

I was thrilled to see her buying a book much more challenging than her previous choices. The extra lessons I was giving her must have been boosting her confidence and ambition, as well as her ability. I scanned the book's barcode, slipped the money in the till, and slid one of our free bookmarks inside the pages before handing it back to her.

"Good choice."

With her hand in her mum's, she was just about to go out of the door when she turned and called over her shoulder to me, "Aren't you coming to the practice, miss? I thought it was your play."

"Sorry, I can't. I have to work here this afternoon. But have fun!"

Hector, who had just finished helping an older boy to find a Tintin book he hadn't already read, came to stand by me at the counter as the shop started to empty. Together we watched our young customers, the smallest ones accompanied by their parents, cross the road to the Village Hall.

"I assumed you'd be going to the rehearsal too, Sophie. Don't tell me you've fallen out with Damian?"

I busied myself with tidying the bookmarks on the counter. "Actually, I hadn't fallen in with him. This is purely a professional arrangement that's been thrust upon me."

Hector winced, making me wish I'd phrased it differently. "Anyway, I thought you'd need me here on a busy Saturday in the run-up to Christmas."

Hector replied quickly. "Oh, I do, Sophie. I'm glad you didn't ask for the time off, to spare me the awkwardness of having to say no." He coughed and walked over to the central display table to add to the stacks of books. With no customers in the shop now, I pulled the duster out from under the counter and headed for the nearest bookshelves. "I expect there'll be a rush on when the rehearsal is over, so I'll just clean and lay up all the tearoom tables while I've got a moment."

"Could you put some more flyers on the tea tables please, Sophie?"

I hadn't really looked at the flyers he'd been printing, but when I read them I got a shock. "I thought you were only opening on Sundays during Advent? It says here that you're starting tomorrow, but it's not even December yet."

Hector flattened the cardboard box from which he'd just replenished the cookery section. "That's right. There are four Sundays in Advent, and the fourth is the one before Christmas Day. This year December the twenty-fifth falls on a Sunday, so if you look at the calendar and work backwards, the first Sunday of Advent is tomorrow."

"But Advent calendars always start on the first of December."

"If you want to change the church calendar, you'll have to take it up with the Archbishop of Canterbury, Sophie. And the new vicar. He's been moving back into the vicarage today, ready to take the first Advent service at St Bride's tomorrow. Shall you go?"

I pondered.

"I wasn't planning to, but maybe I should, given that I want to use his church for my play. I know Kate's given permission on his behalf, but I ought to keep in with him. But won't the shop be open at the same time as the service?" I hoped I'd have an excuse not to go.

Hector shook his head. "We're only open a couple of hours in the afternoon, two till four, so that's no excuse to skip church."

"So you'll go too?"

The door creaked open and Billy walked in. "Who's going where?" He trudged past the display table and sat down heavily on a tearoom chair. "And can I come with you? I'm bored."

I crossed to the tearoom and flicked the switch on the kettle. "Church, Billy. We're talking about going to church tomorrow to welcome Mr Murray."

125

Billy perked up. "What, both of you? You having your banns read?" He aimed a lascivious wink at Hector. "About time too."

I avoided Hector's eye.

"If I were you, young Hector, I wouldn't kick Sophie out of bed either."

He laughed out of all proportion to his joke.

"Billy, you are a complete reprobate," I said, wondering why Hector wasn't leaping to defend my honour.

Billy helped himself to a mince pie from the plate on the tearoom counter without using the serving tongs.

"You think so, girlie? My old ma wouldn't have said so. I was her golden boy, I was, compared to my big brother at least. Dirty Bertie, they used to call him."

Hector confirmed Billy's claim with a nod.

"Hard to believe, I know," said Hector. "But we don't talk about Bertie, do we, Billy?"

He fixed Billy with a meaningful glare. Billy's face fell, and for once I felt sorry for him.

"And what did they call you?" I asked Billy, to change the subject.

Billy sat up straight, looking pleased with himself.

"Billy the Kid. Because I was the little brother, do you see? Always the kid brother. Which I didn't mind one bit. I used to like those old cowboy films. John Wayne, all that sort of thing."

I couldn't quite see Billy as a Wild West hero, or even a Wild West anti-hero. I wasn't sure whether Billy the Kid was a goodie or a baddie. Before I could ask, Hector changed the subject.

"Have you seen Mr Murray yet, Billy?" As churchwarden, Billy was a key player in the local church hierarchy. He was also an itinerant gardener employed at the incumbent vicar's discretion. No wonder he was eager to nurture the relationship.

"Aye," said Billy, looking pleased with himself.

"And what about your gardening?" Hector knew all the ways to Billy's heart.

"Same as usual, plus a few extra hours straight off, to make up for lost time between proper vicars. Our Reverend Murray's a real gent."

Hector started rearranging the children's Christmas books to give more prominence to the Bible stories. "And also a voracious reader, as is his wife," he said, sounding happier now. "What's not to love about the Murrays?"

"I'll let you know when I find out whether he likes my play," I said.

27 Candid Camera

"Here you go, miss, I've got it all on film here for you to see."

Just as dusk was starting to fall, Tommy, video camera in hand, came charging in to the shop, flinging the door back to thud against the wall and admitting a blast of cold air. He was almost breathless with excitement.

He strode over to one of the tearoom tables, set the camera down and opened up the small viewing window to give me a private screening.

I sat down beside Tommy, my hopes raised by his infectious enthusiasm and obvious pride in his achievement.

"I missed out the boring bits when your Damian and those actor people were telling everyone what to do, and I turned it off whenever any of the kids started crying."

"Did that happen a lot?"

Tommy shrugged.

"Well, that's what kids do mostly, isn't it?"

That made me feel sad for his childhood.

"But I did quite a clever thing and took a few shots in the background to create an idea of the atmoph – asthmo – what it felt like."

As his customer left the shop, Hector came over to stand behind me and look over my shoulder. "You've been reading up on this film-making business, then, Tommy?"

Tommy gave Hector his biggest smile. "Yes, cheers, Hector, that book you gave me is brilliant. I've been reading it in bed till two o'clock every night this week."

Hector grimaced. "I'll be in trouble with your mum."

Tommy shook his head reassuringly. "Oh no, don't worry about her, she's asleep by ten every night after her bottle of wine."

"Glass, I think you mean, Tommy, not bottle?" I said hopefully.

"No, bottle. But don't worry, it's only bottles on weeknights. She saves the wine boxes for the weekends. Anyway…"

He pressed a button, keen to get back on track, and the tiny screen whirred into action. The picture jolted a lot, indicating either Tommy's enthusiasm for finding a new and interesting vantage point every minute or so, or his low boredom threshold.

Hector looked in puzzlement at a shot that showed the tops of the infants' heads progressing down the middle of the hall.

"That's a clever angle, Tommy. How did you manage that? It reminds me of the scene on the Ferris wheel in *The Third Man*, where Orson Welles describes people as ants."

I wasn't familiar with the film, but I could see what he meant. I didn't remember seeing a ladder in the Village Hall, and I couldn't imagine any of the adults letting Tommy use one if there had been. Nor was there attic space above the Hall or a loft hatch that might have given him this bird's-eye view.

"I climbed up on the roof and looked down through the skylight, of course. Clever, huh?"

130

The door creaked to admit a middle-aged couple, and Hector went to attend to them.

"The roof? What, on the outside of the roof? How on earth did you get up there?"

"Oh, the usual way." Tommy spoke casually, as if it was something everyone did.

This scene was followed by a blur several seconds long.

"I forgot to pause it while I got down again."

There was a loud scrunch compatible with a teenage boy landing heavily in the large box of sand used to grit the Hall car park in icy weather.

"I very nearly missed the sandbox, but it wouldn't have mattered if I had, because I'd have landed on Damian's van."

I wasn't sure Damian would have seen it that way. The film kept rolling with glimpses of Tommy brushing himself off once he'd straightened up.

"Hang on." I reached out to press the pause button. "I thought you said you stopped filming whenever a child started crying?"

"Yes, that's right, miss. It's called editing."

I pressed rewind briefly, then play. "But I'm sure I heard the sound of a child crying then."

We both listened intently and I caught a muffled wailing that sounded as if it was coming from the inside of the van. Tommy was the first to make sense of it.

"Oh no, miss, that's not a child. That's a baby. New babies make a different sort of noise to children, sort of high-pitched and miserable."

I shook my head.

"No, it can't be. Why would Damian have a baby in his van?"

Tommy thought for a moment. "Are you sure it's Damian's van? There was another van like his in the car park earlier."

"Surely you can tell them apart? Damian's has got loads of stickers and writing on it."

"Yes, but not on the roof. From above both vans look exactly the same."

Tommy brightened. "I know. I bet that baby's a prop for the play. Come to think of it, they never did get out a real Baby Jesus. They were just using a Baby Annabell doll, like my little sister's got. I guess that was just a stunt double."

Hector joined us for a moment while the couple continued to browse. "Jesus would be too big a star to get involved till everyone's word perfect," he said, deadpan. I slapped him on the thigh for his irreverence, but Tommy nodded.

"That reminds me, I stopped filming whenever anyone couldn't remember their lines."

The video immediately jumped forward to the final tableau, with everyone frozen in position for dramatic effect. Tommy tapped the Angel Gabriel. "She's out. She was first to move."

For all his teenage swaggering, Tommy was not long out of primary school himself, and of an age at which he might still have enjoyed a game of musical statues at birthday parties. He probably would have liked a part in the play, too.

I looked at the tearoom clock. By my calculation, the video had lasted about four minutes, including Tommy's tumble from the roof. I gritted my teeth behind my smile, telling myself not to worry, this was the children's first rehearsal.

I coughed and tried to pull myself together, then realised Tommy was watching me hopefully for my verdict.

"Thank you very much, Tommy," I said. "It's kind of you to give up your Saturday afternoon for this. I think he's earned a free milkshake, don't you, Hector?"

I didn't want to overstretch Hector's generosity, realising he'd already given Tommy a book about film making, but Hector didn't seem to mind. He told me later the book was another of his car boot sale bargains.

When Tommy finally left, just in time for us to shut up shop for the night, Hector and I looked at each other in silence for a moment, then burst out laughing.

"Orson Welles, eat your heart out," said Hector. Although I was embarrassed to have to ask whether Orson was a boy's name or a girl's name, I was glad I did, because it immediately led Hector to invite me to spend the evening watching *The Third Man* on DVD in his flat. But even its jaunty zither theme music could not drown out the mysterious baby's crying playing on a loop in my head.

28 Welcome Back, Vicar

"What should I wear to church?" I asked Hector next morning, throwing back the duvet.

"A bit more than that. Though your current outfit would certainly make you stand out from the crowd."

"But should I wear a dress or a skirt?" Sitting on the edge of the bed, I slipped into the emerald silk dressing gown that had been hanging on the back of his bedroom door.

Hector closed his eyes. "I'm probably not the best person to ask. You could always phone Kate for advice. She's good with frocks." He pointed lazily to the phone on the bedside table.

"And have her see that I'm phoning from your flat's landline first thing in the morning? I don't want to encourage her."

Hector straightened the duvet. "Good point. But don't worry. The Reverend Murray won't care what you're wearing. He won't judge you by your clothes, any more than God would, if you believed in him."

I opened Hector's sock drawer and selected a soft pale blue pair to borrow, wondering whether vicars always had to wear black socks.

"It's all very well for vicars. They don't have to worry about what to wear. It's like being a policeman or a fireman. Their outfits are like a uniform, same as God. I mean, always the long white robe."

Hector opened his eyes, sat up, punched his pillow into shape and positioned it behind his back for comfort. "You want a bookshop uniform? I could have fun choosing one for you."

Now I thought about it, Hector did have his own uniform for the shop: jeans, t-shirt and fleece or sweater. I gave him a playful thump.

"I don't know why I'm asking you for fashion advice, anyway, seeing you always wear the same thing. I'll call for you on my way back up to church at half past nine."

As I walked up my garden path, trying to decide between my businesslike navy blue interview dress and a softer rose pink tunic, Joshua was trying to put something into the wheelie bin outside his front door. He was juggling his walking stick in one hand, the rubbish bag in the other. I leaned over the low lavender hedge between our front paths to hold the lid open to make it easier for him.

Relieved of his burden, he raised his tweed cap to me. No-one had ever raised their hat to me before I met Joshua, and I found it charming.

"Good morning, my dear. Have you been up early to fetch the Sunday paper?" From the twinkle in his eye, I suspected he was teasing me, as I clearly didn't have a Sunday newspaper in my possession. I quickly changed the subject.

"Joshua! The very person! I was just wondering what to wear to church this morning. I thought I'd go and meet the Reverend Murray, but as I never go to church, I wasn't sure of the etiquette. Do you think I should wear a dress?"

He looked down at my jeans with amusement. "Always. Besides, it would be courteous to Mr Murray to dress up a little to welcome him back this morning."

"Honestly, I know embarrassingly little about church form. I didn't even know the first Sunday in Advent could fall in November. I thought that would be like having August Bank Holiday in July." I sighed. "I've still so much to learn about village life."

Joshua leaned on his stick with both hands. "Give it a year, my dear. When you've seen the whole cycle of village life once through, you'll feel much better. Go and change into your best frock now, and we can walk up to church together presently."

Going at his pace would mean leaving ten minutes earlier than I'd planned, so I dashed inside, grabbed the first respectable dress I could find in the wardrobe, swapped Hector's socks for tights, and slicked on a quick touch of make-up. Then I pulled my phone from the pocket of my discarded jeans and sent Hector a quick text of warning.

"Walking up to church with Joshua. Pretend we haven't spent the night together. Sx."

The reply came just as I was about to head out of the door.

"OK, you and Joshua haven't spent the night together. I should hope not indeed. Hx."

When I left the house, slipping into my winter coat as I closed the front door, Joshua was already on the path, leaning on his stick waiting for me. We chatted as we walked up the High Street at his leisurely pace.

"So if today's the first Sunday in Advent, should I be putting up the Christmas decorations in my cottage?" I had got into the habit of consulting Joshua as if he were the Siri of village life.

"Dear me, no." He sounded shocked. "If you want to do things traditionally, you should be doing that on Christmas Eve. And taking them down on Twelfth Night. You don't want to have evergreens in the house too long, it's bad luck."

I didn't like to tell him that I'd been thinking more along the lines of tinsel and fairy lights. He pointed his stick at the undecorated window of the village shop as we passed. "You see? Carol shows the correct decorum, unlike the big stores down in Slate Green."

"Then I shan't feel very Christmassy for ages yet, unless I'm at work."

"But what about your nativity play?"

How foolish of me not to have counted that as festive.

"Of course, not everyone in the village shares my views about decorations," Joshua said, as we approached Hector's House. Hector emerged from his flat, feigning a look of surprise.

"Good morning, Sophie, Joshua. Heading my way?" he asked innocently, and quickly fell into step with us.

29 Sunday Service

Hector and I weren't the only heathens heading to church to welcome the Reverend Murray back to the village – or to meet him for the first time, in my case. The High Street was as busy as during the school run.

"He won't get this big a congregation every Sunday," said Joshua, sadly.

The moment I saw the Reverend Murray, I liked him. He had clearly mastered the art of the charm offensive, putting newcomers like me at our ease. A dapper, slightly paunchy man in his mid-sixties, he had a generous air about him, and gave the impression of one who enjoyed all that life had to offer. As we left the church after the service, his wife stood beside him, smiling gently and making confident eye contact with all comers. She was a gently rounded woman in a neat skirt suit and plain dove grey velvet beret, with a large mauve woollen shawl arranged about her shoulders for draughtproofing. They made a tidy pair, reminding me of the little people in a weather house, only both allowed out at the same time.

As we lined up to shake their hands, Billy, in his churchwarden's robe, pottered about in the background, stacking the hymn books and service sheets. He looked unusually tidy himself, as if some of the Murrays' neatness had rubbed off on him already.

Kate queue-jumped to join us. "Vicar, you haven't yet met Hector's partner Sophie. She's May Sayers's great-niece and now works in his bookshop."

Mr Murray clasped my hand with both of his in a warm welcome, reminding me that although I'd lived here six months now, I was still regarded as a newcomer.

"You must come and have a glass of sherry with us one evening," he invited.

"Or coffee, Gerard," said his wife gently. "There's always coffee."

I suppressed a smile.

"Are you free this afternoon?" asked Hector. "We're opening Sunday afternoons during Advent, as usual, just for a couple of hours."

"That's right, keep Sunday special," said the vicar cheerfully. I realised he was admonishing Hector for trading on the Sabbath, but in the gentlest possible manner.

"I'm afraid we can't join you this afternoon, Hector," said Mrs Murray, lingering over her handshake with him. "We have guests for Sunday lunch. But we will come and visit you in the shop as soon as we can. I've missed you, you know. There's no proper bookshop within miles of our retirement cottage."

Hector leaned in towards her, his arms perhaps aching as she'd been holding on to him for so long. "I can always do mail order, you know."

"I don't think my husband would approve of me ordering a male," she said, winking shamelessly.

Hector chuckled as he withdrew his hands.

"It's good to have you both back in Wendlebury, though of course under circumstances none of us would have chosen."

Mr Murray's planned replacement had gone on long-term sick leave.

Mr Murray beamed at me, oblivious to his wife's flirtatious behaviour. "I do love a good book. And not just The Good Book, ha ha."

As we walked down the path through the lychgate and regained the High Street, I recalled our own plans for the afternoon.

"Maybe it's just as well they're not coming, or they'd see their churchwarden playing Santa."

Hector took my hand. "No problem there. Billy's got no secrets from the vicar that I know of. Besides, Santa Claus was originally a Christian figure – Sinterklaas or Saint Nicholas."

"Yes, accompanied by a demonic sidekick, Zwarte Piet," I said, remembering the legend still popular in the Netherlands, where I spent a year during my peripatetic teaching career.

I glanced back at the vicar and his wife, still standing in the church porch chatting to the parishioners. "Still, given a choice, I think I'd rather have the vicar down my chimney than Billy."

30 Santa Baby

"Why didn't Santa's reindeer bring him?" asked a small boy as the pony trap turned into the High Street from the lane down to Stanley's farm.

Hector had his answers already prepared.

"He only uses them on Christmas Eve when his sleigh's really heavy, laden with presents for the whole world. The donkey's plenty big enough to bring special pre-Christmas presents just for Wendlebury children today."

"But that's not a sleigh," persisted the child. "It's got wheels."

Hector tutted. "Have you ever heard of Chitty Chitty Bang Bang? You know, the car that can float like a boat or fly in the sky?"

The little boy nodded, wide-eyed.

"It was modelled on Santa's sleigh."

The little boy turned to his father. "Dad, can I have a sleigh like that for Christmas?"

Hector slipped away into the shop before he could hear the answer.

As Billy got closer, the crowd started cheering. When he drew to a halt outside the shop, they clamoured around him eagerly.

"Whoa, Janet," Billy called out, one of the few lines he was allowed as part of his act. Hector had been drilling him all week to stick to innocuous comments such as: "What would you like for Christmas?", "Make sure you tell your mummy and daddy too," "Have you been good this year?", "And how old are you?", "Good boy", "Good girl", and "Well done".

I had to admire Hector's format for the afternoon. While most stores tuck their Father Christmas away in a grotto, Hector said he liked to keep him out in the open for all to enjoy the spectacle. This meant he could keep an eye on him.

So Billy sat in state in a corner of the shop on a wooden throne borrowed from the church, while the children queued through the shop for their turn to meet him. On no account were any children allowed to sit on his knee. Not that Hector believed Billy would do anything inappropriate. He just wanted to guard against complaints. Instead, a low wooden stool from the stockroom was placed at Santa's side to serve as a child-sized seat.

Some of the parents sat out the wait in the tearoom, while others browsed the bookshelves. Those in the tearoom bought refreshments to justify their seats, so I was kept busy serving drinks and cakes all afternoon. Meanwhile Hector served a steady stream of customers at the trade counter, selling tickets to see Santa at two pounds apiece, as well as a sizeable quantity of books.

Billy sat with his back to the tearoom, a pile of Advent calendars on a low table beside him. I could see the children's faces as they took their turn on the footstool, mostly rapt with wonder at the apparition in red. Even the most boisterous became subdued, their voices breathy, as they reported on their behaviour. Visiting Santa must have felt like a job interview to them, or a viva in which the price of failure was high.

31 She's A Believer

Towards closing time, as the queue was starting to wane, the shop door swung open and Tommy Crowe walked in, accompanied by a sandy-haired girl of about ten. I recognised her from the fireworks party. Bright-eyed, she presented a two-pound coin to Hector, before heading straight to Santa's corner, jigging about excitedly as she awaited her turn.

"I'll be talking to my friend, Sina," Tommy called after her, heading for the tearoom. I glanced around the tables for any customers of his own age and found none.

"My little sister," he said to me grimly, jabbing his thumb over his shoulder towards her, before leaning on the cake counter, as if settling down for a chat with me.

"What's her name again?" I asked. "I didn't quite catch it."

Tommy tutted and rolled his eyes, leaving Hector to answer on his behalf. "Sina, short for Thomasina."

"Like my name, only more of it," said Tommy bitterly. "She got three more letters than I did."

I avoided Hector's eye, too intrigued not to pursue this line of questioning. "So Tommy is short for Thomas?"

Tommy nodded. "Yeah. My mum called both of us after my dad. But he still left."

Embarrassed to have probed a sensitive spot of his unfortunate family history, I tried to make light of it.

"Gosh, good thing there weren't three of you, or she'd have run out of names."

I hadn't realised Thomasina had tuned into our conversation from her place at the front of the queue.

"But there might be," she called across the shop. "Mum's going to have another baby."

"No, she's not," said Tommy quickly.

"She'll have to if I ask Santa to give her one for Christmas," retorted Sina in clear, high tones. "But I don't know what she'll call it."

The whole shop had fallen quiet.

"How about Tomato?" said Santa, dispatching a little boy in a Spiderman t-shirt.

A few shoppers sniggered.

"Or Tombola?" Santa was playing to the gallery now.

"Or Tomintoul." A note of warning in his voice, Hector cited the brand name of the bottle of Scotch hidden under the counter, Billy's reward for his Santa performance, on the condition that it went off without adverse incident. Billy immediately reverted to his agreed dialogue.

Tommy moved on to his favourite topic of the moment. Strolling over to the trade counter, he pulled his video camera out of his parka pocket.

"Hector, do you want me to film Santa for you?" He uncapped the lens and pressed the on button. "Or is he like vampires and won't show up in films?"

"You're thinking of mirrors, Tommy," said Hector. "I'm pretty sure you can safely capture Santa on film. But not with the children, unless you've got their parents' permission."

"I don't know where my dad is to ask him, so I can't film Sina."

"Just your mum's consent would do for Sina, Tommy." Hector's voice was gentle. "And if Sina doesn't mind, of course."

Tommy peered at Santa through the viewfinder, and the camera whirred into action. Sina immediately became louder and more animated, as if her 'on' button had also been pressed. Putting the camera to his eye, Tommy walked slowly over to Santa's corner, impervious to the display table and rack of greeting cards that he bumped into on the way.

The tearoom orders had petered out now, so I went to help Hector, gift-wrapping the books he was putting through the till.

At four o'clock precisely, just as I was starting to think my fingers would be raw if I had to handle any more Sellotape, Hector switched off the Christmas music on the CD player to indicate closing time. The last few customers besides Tommy and Sina took the hint and left, and I started cleaning the tearoom tables. Santa got up, stretched, and helped himself to half a mince pie that some absent-minded customer had left on a bookshelf.

Tommy set up his camera on the trade counter to show Hector his recording, and Billy and I went to join them. Sina wriggled under Tommy's arm to get a prime view of the action replay of her receiving Santa's gift. Both Santa and Sina were smiling stiffly at the camera as she moved in to take her turn on the footstool. Billy was clearly doing his best to adhere to his agreed script while the evidence was being captured on film.

"So, Sina Crowe, what's your name?"

"My name is Sina Crowe, Santa, what's yours?"

Billy very nearly said, "Billy," turning the initial B into our "bless you, my child", as if reverting to Santa's saintly origins. His follow-up was a welcome distraction. "And have you been a good girl?"

Sina's exaggerated look of innocence made me suspect she had not. "Yes, and my brother has too, so can he have a present as well, please?"

"On Christmas Day he can. Unless he's got two quid on him now."

Santa put his hand protectively over his diminishing pile of Advent calendars. Sina scowled.

"Mum only had enough money for one. And she said Tommy is too old for one now anyway."

"Rules is rules," returned Billy. "I'm just doing my job, girlie."

Sina was not one to be cowed by authority. "Yes, but surely you make the rules, Santa? I mean, you're like the King of Christmas."

I gathered Tommy's household was not strictly religious.

"So why can't you just give one to my brother anyway? He'd really like one for his bedroom."

She stood up, bringing her own tousled head to the same height as Santa's, her fists clenched before her chest.

"You've got loads left over. I'm last in the queue." She cast an arm around the empty space behind her. "Surely it would be easier not to take them all back to the North Pole? So here's the deal: give one to me, one to my brother, and the rest to Hector for his shop. After all, he's been kind enough to let you in to his shop to shelter out of the cold for a couple of hours."

It looked as if, in his head, Santa was running through his stock of acceptable replies.

"And Merry Christmas to you," he came up with eventually. Taking two envelopes from the pile, he held them out to Sina at arm's length, like a string of garlic before a vampire. With a satisfied smile that seemed to say, "My work here is done", she took them both, hugged them close to her chest, and without more ado marched away from Santa towards the camera to rejoin her brother.

Tommy clicked the off button and looked anxiously at Hector, craving approval.

"Well done, Tommy, and thanks," said Hector. "And you too, Sina."

"And thanks to Billy, too," said Tommy, which was thoughtful of him.

Billy looked startled at the sound of his real name, as if he thought his cover was blown. Sina tucked the calendars under one arm and slipped her hand into Tommy's.

"Oh Tommy, you are funny. How could Billy possibly be Santa? Billy's far too stupid and lazy. I mean, he can't even fly. Come on, let's go home and open all the doors on our calendars."

"But—" I was about to admonish them, then I stopped. If that made them happy, who was I to interfere?

The door banged behind them, and for a moment all was peaceful. Billy was the first to break the silence.

"Now, let's be having that Tomintoul, young Hector. It's the closest I'm going to get to flying today."

32 The Holly and the Ivy

"What you need to set your window display off a treat is a nice bit of fresh mistletoe."

Busy arranging ceramic figures in a nativity scene in the bookshop window, I looked round to see who had spoken. A trail of muddy wellington boot prints from door to counter led me to Billy, standing partially camouflaged by a huge bunch of evergreens. I set down a china shepherd beside its sheep and turned to face him.

"I don't think so, Billy, thank you all the same. Live greenery dripping sap and spiders isn't a great asset to a bookshop. Besides, I don't think mistletoe really goes with a manger scene. That would seem rather bad taste."

I also didn't fancy being with Billy near mistletoe, though I wouldn't have minded if Hector bought some for his flat.

"But it's very reasonably priced at just a fiver a bunch. Prices will rise nearer Christmas, and it might get scarce due to excessive demand." He held out a sprig of mistletoe as if tempting Janet, the donkey, with a carrot. "Everyone in the village will be wanting it today, so they can get their houses done up ready for the tree lights being switched on tomorrow night. You'd better get some while you can."

A knock on the shop window nearly hard enough to break the glass drew my attention to Tommy, standing guard outside over a rusting wheelbarrow brimming with festive greenery.

"How about some holly and ivy instead?" Billy tried again. "You can't disapprove of holly and ivy, because they're in a Christmas carol. That makes them holy, more or less."

The shop door creaked open to admit Hector, half hidden behind a large potted Christmas tree he'd been to fetch from the garden centre in Slate Green.

"What's all this, Birnam Wood moving to Dunsinane?" I asked, eager to make a literary reference.

Smiling at me approvingly through the uppermost branches, Hector kicked the door closed behind him to stop the rush of cold air that had accompanied him. He nodded towards Billy.

"It rather looks like Pogles' Wood has beaten Birnam Wood to it."

Billy offered up a dripping sprig of holly, like a gypsy pressing lucky heather upon a reluctant stranger.

"I've brought the perfect complement to your Christmas tree, young Hector," he said. "What could be more Christmassy than a bit of holly?"

"I could say turkeys, but that doesn't mean I want either of them messing up my nice, clean shop."

Hector lowered the pot to the floor beside the counter and took off his coat, releasing a shower of loose pine needles to mingle with the mud on the floor.

"Whose woods have you been raiding this time, Billy?"

Billy bridled.

"I had Stanley's permission. You can ask him if you don't believe me."

Affronted, he turned his back on Hector and tried me again.

"Well, how about some offcuts to put in those little posy vases on your tearoom tables? I can do you a big handful of holly, ivy and mistletoe trimmings for a couple of quid."

He pointed through the window to the barrow, and Hector peered through the glass to inspect its load.

"Actually, I wouldn't mind a decent sized bit of mistletoe."

Billy pursed his lips.

"Carol took the best of it to hang inside the shop door. She doesn't usually put any evergreens up at Christmas, so I reckon she must have someone special in her sights this year. You better look out next time you're up there, young Hector."

Hector grimaced. "I don't think she's after me any more, Billy."

I made a mental note to make sure Billy wasn't in the village shop next time I visited.

Hector reached a hand into his jeans pocket, pulled out a two-pound coin and handed it to Billy. "But let Sophie choose which bits she wants. I don't want any rubbish."

Billy jerked his thumb in Tommy's direction. "On you go then, girlie. Let the boy show you what we've got. And don't go sweet-talking him into giving you more than two quid's worth either."

I collected an empty tray from the tearoom, swung the shop door open and was met by a big smile from Tommy.

I picked carefully through the shorter branches, trying to avoid pricking my fingers on holly leaves as I searched for sprigs with lots of berries. The mistletoe berries, slightly damp from the drizzle outside, glistened, pearlescent. Trying to remember whether they were poisonous, I thought I'd better look them up in one of

May's gardening books before putting them in vases on the tearoom tables. I could imagine a toddler mistaking them for sweets.

"I hope Billy's not taking advantage of you in his little venture," I said, piling the best bits up on my tray.

Tommy was wide-eyed. "Oh no, miss, he's letting me have all the fun. Climbing the trees with the saw to cut the branches down, chopping them down to size when I'm back on the ground, pushing the barrow—"

"And what's left for Billy to do, exactly?" I shuddered at this health and safety nightmare.

"He looks after the money side of things, which is fine by me. I hate maths. This isn't meant to be like homework."

"And have you sold much?"

Tommy threw back his shoulders with pride. "This is our third barrow full, and we've only done one side of the High Street so far."

"I don't suppose you've got a side line in fairy lights? I've just realised I haven't got any for my cottage yet."

"Oh no, miss, just the greenery. Because we can get all that stuff for free. It's pure profit, see?"

Yes, I saw, but I wondered how little of the profit ended up in Tommy's pocket. I decided to have a word with Billy out of Tommy's earshot later, to make sure. I suspected a bit of pocket money would make a big difference to Tommy, whereas Billy would just spend the lot in the pub.

My tea-tray fully loaded, I thanked Tommy and was just turning to go back indoors when he grabbed at my sleeve.

"Miss, will you help me do something tomorrow?"

I knew Tommy better than to commit myself without further enquiry. "Does it involve climbing trees with sharp implements?"

He grinned, apparently glad of the distraction from his real request. It took him a moment to spit it out.

"Will you help me choose some Christmas presents in the bookshop? I mean, I'm not much good at knowing what to get my mum and my sister, but I really want to get something they'll like." He frowned. "And now it looks as if I might have to buy something for a baby too. I know babies can't read when they're born, but I thought maybe one of those hard books with no words in might make a good Christmas present for a baby."

"It can't be that hard if there are no words," I said, wondering whether he'd get the joke. He didn't.

"Not hard to read. Just hard. You know, the sort of books that babies can chew."

"You mean board books." I smiled. "Yes, of course, Tommy. I'll help you choose a good one, if you like. And I'll get Billy to leave some money with Hector from what you've earned so far, to make sure you've got enough for what you want to buy."

Tommy beamed. "Thanks, miss. You're all right, you are."

I slipped back into the shop, blocking Billy's exit until I'd extracted thirty pounds from him on Tommy's behalf. I watched them wander back up the High Street together, Tommy eagerly pushing the barrow, Billy thumbing through his remaining roll of banknotes. Then I turned round one of our little books on babies' names to display the cover as a hint to Tommy's mother, just in case she happened to call in before her baby was due.

33 Second Time Lucky

"Why don't we hold a book swap party after Christmas, so that children can come in and exchange books they have been given for Christmas but don't like?"

Replenishing the children's classics section, I had a flashback to receiving three copies of *Little Women* at Christmas when I was ten. At that age, that was three too many, and it had put me off reading the book ever since.

"That sounds a good idea, Sophie," said a mother, placing a five-pound note and a box of Christmas cards on the counter. "Something free to look forward to after Christmas. Can you do it for adults too, Hector?"

Her husband came up behind her. "A bit like swinging, eh, Hector?" He winked behind her back. She turned around to acknowledge him.

"I think you mean swishing, darling. Like clothes-swapping parties."

"I know what I mean, love." He patted her bottom as I gave her a pound and a penny change.

I turned, wide-eyed, to Hector, as they left the shop. "Gosh, is there anything that doesn't happen in Wendlebury Barrow?"

"I'd be the last to know about that one," he said. "Though if it doesn't happen in Wendlebury Barrow, it's probably not worth doing. But I think your book swap idea is a good one, provided they only swap with each other's books, and not with our stock. I doubt any books would be in saleable condition after being in sticky hands on Christmas Day."

As I went to serve some customers waiting in the tearoom, I kept an eye open for husbands or wives changing tables, but was disappointed.

I'd almost forgotten about the nativity play rehearsal taking place at the Village Hall until just after four o'clock, when Tommy made his characteristic noisy and breathless entrance into the shop.

"Want to see this week's film?" he asked hopefully. I was nervous of seeing the evidence after last week's showing, but he looked so earnest that I didn't have the heart to say no.

"OK," I said tentatively. "Will it take longer than last week?" I rather hoped so, or else it meant no-one had learned their lines, and the children had spent the afternoon crying.

Tommy scraped a chair out from under a table and spun it round to sit on it back to front, balancing on the back (now front) two legs only. I was about to caution him, when I realised that if he could climb trees holding sharp instruments and jump off the Village Hall roof without damaging himself, he was probably indestructible. He pushed the sugar bowl and milk jug out of his way to clear a space for his camera.

Hector remained at the till while customers were in the shop, then came over to join us when the video was half way through. So far, it was running surprisingly well, with no forgotten lines or upset children.

"Of course, they don't look like much without their costumes," said Tommy, narrowing his eyes critically. "But Damian said Carol will have them all done in time for next week."

I clutched one hand to my chest. "That's a relief. I'm glad he's persuaded her to make them after all. I was worried she might refuse, as the play's about Christmas."

Hector raised his eyebrows. "Is she making the costumes for the whole cast? That's over a hundred people. That's a tall order."

"Most of the kids are short," said Tommy. "Anyway, any of them who have got an animal onesie at home are being allowed to use that as their costume."

"Surely they're not all sheep onesies?"

I had a horrible feeling the chief shepherd might end up looking like Noah.

Tommy shrugged. "I dunno. Besides, the shepherds only need dressing gowns and tea towels on their heads. So Carol hasn't got to make that many."

At that point in the filming, Tommy must have got bored, as he'd started to pan round the hall.

"Look, Damian brought some of the costumes to show us."

The camera zoomed in on an apparent sea of feathers nestling in the corner of the hall.

Hector burst out laughing. "My God, it's Mother Goose! Is one of the three wise men bringing a golden egg?"

I clapped my hands over my eyes. "Oh, my goodness, don't joke, Hector. I hope Carol isn't going over the top."

Even this extraordinary sight didn't hold Tommy's attention for long, and he continued to turn the camera about. Next, he stopped to focus on the glass panel in the door that led in from the lobby, where a hooded face was pressed to the glass, looking in.

"Bloody hell, I didn't notice her the first time around," said Tommy. "Who do you think that is? A ghost?"

"Why a ghost?" I asked. "I've never heard of the Village Hall being haunted."

"It's probably just someone's mum sneaking a look to see how her child is getting on," said the practical Hector.

Tommy looked up in surprise, as if Hector's was the more outlandish suggestion. "Well, you get ghosts at Christmas, don't you?"

Hector frowned. "What, like the Ghost of Christmas Past?"

Tommy acknowledged Hector's suggestion with a sweep of his arm, jogging the table enough to make the camera wobble. "There, you see, Sophie, Hector knows what I'm talking about. And anyway, I didn't notice it when I was filming. It's just like those programmes you see on the telly, where they set up cameras to film haunted houses and no-one sees the ghost until after the film's been developed."

"It's called Photoshop, Tommy," said Hector gently, returning to the counter.

Tommy was undaunted. "No, it's definitely a ghost. Which explains why I heard more of those weird baby crying noises from that van this afternoon."

"So the ghost drives a van?" asked Hector. "That'll give the Ghostbusters a run for their money."

"No, it's Damian's van," said Tommy. "I think it must be haunted. Now I've seen this ghost, I think it must be the mother of the baby, and the baby in Damian's van is a baby ghost."

"Are you sure it was Damian's van?" I asked, doubtfully. "It could have been the other white van that was in the car park last week when you heard it."

I glanced across to Hector to gauge his reaction, but he had his head down, cashing up for the night. Tommy raised his hands defensively.

"Don't blame me. I'm just the cameraman."

I looked back at the screen for further evidence, only to see Tommy had spent the next twenty seconds focusing on a pile of donkey droppings on the wooden parquet floor. They were definitely not in my script either.

34 Lights!

As I stood outside The Bluebird in the dark, trying to spot Hector amongst the crowd, a stocky figure in a duffle coat sidled up to me. It wore a bobble hat covered with mistletoe, topped with an old bicycle lamp tied on with string. In its hand was a pint glass spilling over with mulled wine. Its growly voice startled me.

"Good evening, girlie."

It was Billy. He pointed to his hat.

"Got a Christmas kiss for your old friend tonight?"

To my relief, at that precise moment Hector came jostling through the crowd, wearing an ancient deerstalker and a thick stripy scarf over a long overcoat. I was beginning to wonder whether I'd missed the notice for fancy dress to be worn.

"Do I detect unrest?" was his greeting to me.

I grinned.

"Nice hat, Sherlock."

He touched it appreciatively.

"I've had it since I was a teenager. It came from my parents' antique shop. It's so battered that I only bring it out in the dark when you can't see the moth holes. But I'm very attached to it."

"Can I be your Dr Watson?"

"Wouldn't you rather be Mrs Hudson? You do make a fine cup of tea."

I batted his arm for teasing me, but before I could protest further, a slight figure dressed entirely in black bowled up to join us, a sinister balaclava covering all of its face but the eyes. Alarmed, I took a step back, but Hector was not worried.

"Hello, Tommy."

Tommy pulled off the balaclava and stuffed it crossly into his pocket.

"How did you know it was me?"

Hector tapped his deerstalker. "Sherlock Holmes says you can never disguise a back."

"But this is my front."

Tommy stomped off, pulling his video camera out of his other pocket as he went. I surveyed the crowd as it absorbed him.

"Gosh, I'd forgotten quite how many people live here."

I reached into my coat pocket to pull out the pile of invitations to the Wendlebury Writers' book launch. The lighting-up ceremony provided the perfect opportunity to distribute them to villagers without having to go door-to-door. I wondered where to start.

"I suppose these are all villagers."

Hector nodded.

"Most of them, as far as I can tell, although I suspect a few usually come up from Slate Green to get their hands on some free mulled wine. Word gets around about such things." He pulled his scarf a little closer around his neck, and I looped my arm through his to snuggle closer.

"I'm surprised how many villagers I know now. And it's nice to no longer be the newest person in town. I can see at least one person who wasn't even born when I moved into my cottage."

I pointed to a tiny baby in the arms of a slight lone female standing on the edge of the crowd. The mother, hood up, head bowed, was completely engrossed in her baby's company, holding its hands and talking to it, as if there was no-one else around. I wondered whether she was as much a newcomer to the village as the baby. Perhaps she was painfully shy. There was no father in evidence, and of all the crowd, she seemed to be the only one not mingling with others.

"She looks a bit lonely and awkward," I said. "I don't know who she is, but there's something familiar about her. Why does she remind me of Billy? No, hang on, she's more like Carol, only a young, pretty version."

Hector laughed. "Everyone looks the same on a dark night like this, all bundled up against the cold. It's easier to recognise people in their Halloween outfits."

He turned around to check her out, and gazed at the woman for so long that I felt uncomfortable. I didn't think she was that good-looking.

"Actually I don't know who she is either," he said at last. "I wonder whether she's a traveller? They congregate down on Slate Common now and again, until the council gets the police to move them on. I hadn't heard they were back."

I wanted him to return his attention to me.

"So what happens now?" I asked.

"I'll show you."

He took my hand and led me through the crowd to a trestle table outside the pub, where Donald and his wife were busy ladling mulled wine into polystyrene cups.

"First, we all have some of this, on the house." He picked up two full cups and handed one to me. "Then we all assemble round the Christmas tree on the green, where the youngest child in the school and the oldest person in the village do the ceremonial switching on of the tree lights. It's a big honour."

I thought about this for a moment.

"Has anyone ever hung around long enough to have done both?" I asked.

"Good question, Sophie. If you ask Bella, as the parish clerk, she'll be able to look it up in the council archives and tell you."

As they collected their mulled wine, people began to surge away from the pub towards the green. Nobody took the most direct route, but wove in and out as they talked to each other. The sight put me in mind of a murmuration of starlings at dusk.

"Has anyone ever been the oldest person in the village for more than a year?" I asked. "I don't think I'd fancy being the chosen one. It would feel like stepping to the front of the queue for the village graveyard."

Hector steered us expertly into a place at the inner edge of the throng, now arranging itself in a circle around the green. "I think the record was five times for one old lady when I was a child. I was starting to think she was immortal, some kind of witch. She even survived the lights fusing the fifth time she switched them on."

"Maybe the power surge recharged her batteries."

Wondering who would be the oldest and youngest this year, I was surprised when Billy stepped forward, along with a very small boy in a snowsuit and Thomas the Tank Engine wellies.

"I thought Joshua was older than Billy?" I said in a low voice to Hector as a hush fell over the crowd.

"Yes, but he's not up to this kind of outing at night. Didn't you read his message in the parish magazine delegating his duty to Billy?"

I chided myself for still not reading it from cover to cover, as it was the highest authority on village news.

The Reverend Murray stepped into the centre of the circle, with Mrs Murray, neat and smiling, at his side. Several people in the front row turned torches on him, during his brief speech of welcome, thanking The Bluebird for its hospitality and the team of dads who had put up the tree and the lights.

His words fell away in the cold night air, punctuated by puffs of vapour emanating from his mouth. When he stopped speaking, everyone clapped, and those who'd come early to the mulled wine whooped and cheered.

When the shouting died down to a respectful silence, the vicar pronounced a formal blessing on the ceremony and made a sign of the cross in the direction of the Christmas tree.

Finally, he beckoned to Billy and the little boy to step up to a large metal box at the foot of the tree. He lifted the lid to reveal a big red handle. I moved closer to Hector.

Billy reached first to the little boy, holding out his hand.

"Come along, Davy, you hold on to old Billy's hand, and we'll do this together."

The little boy shook his head and backed away a step or two. Perhaps the sight of the red handle reminded him of the bomb detonator so often featured in cartoons.

Billy shrugged. "Suit yourself, then." I heard his knees crack as he bent down to reach the handle. He grabbed it, then stood stock still, waiting, familiar with the drill after witnessing the process for scores of years.

"Torches off now, folks, please!" said Mr Murray. "Now let's have the countdown. Five, four, three…"

At zero, there was a split second of expectant hush. Then BANG! But the Christmas tree lights remained dark.

35 Water and Wine

A collective gasp from the crowd sent puffs of vapour scudding about like tiny low clouds, while those with torches or torch apps on their phones turned them in the direction of the noise.

Poor Davy burst into tears and ran back to his dad, who hoisted the little boy on to his shoulders for safety, leaving Billy lying on his back like a stranded beetle, arms and legs flailing. I was glad to see he was still alive.

I was surprised no other children were crying, not even the baby. I turned my head to see how it was faring, but, with its mother, it had vanished into thin air.

Mr and Mrs Murray shot over to Billy's rescue, grabbed his hands and hauled him back to his feet. Then they stood, each with an arm protectively about him, as if fearing he might keel over again like a ninepin, while Trevor came rushing up to check the switch.

"It's all wet. As if someone had just tipped a glass of water over it. It looks like sabotage to me."

He pulled a handful of tissues out of the pocket of his waterproof and swabbed the red handle until it was completely dry.

"But who would do a thing like that?" asked the vicar. "Who would spoil a harmless bit of Christmas fun?"

I thought of Carol, conspicuous by her absence. Had her dislike of Christmas festered to such a level that she wanted no-one else to enjoy it? She could easily have sneaked across from the shop with a bucket of water while everyone was at home getting ready to come out. Or it might have been that lone young mother. There was definitely something odd about her. Perhaps she was the type of misfit that begrudges other people's happiness and wants to spoil it.

"Are you sure it's not just spilled mulled wine?" asked Mrs Murray.

"That would seem more likely," said the vicar.

"I wish I could turn water into wine," said Billy.

Trevor stuffed the soggy tissues back into his pocket.

"Bloody nuisance, whatever it is," he said, wiping his hands on his trousers to dry them. "But I've given it a good dry, so it's perfectly safe, and it should work now. Let's have another go. You up for another crack at it, Davy?"

The little boy, wide-eyed, shook his head.

"Let's leave it to Billy," said his dad. "At least he wasn't earthed. Davy's boots are only plastic, but Billy's are the real McCoy."

"No, they're not, they're rubber," said Billy, hauling himself up from the bench to stride defiantly back to the switch. "You lot going to give me another countdown?"

The masses obeyed, louder and more shrilly than before. I braced myself for another bang, but this time the only noise was the ripple of appreciative "ooohs" that permeated the crowd as the tree lights flickered into life. Then such a huge cheer was raised for the organising committee that you'd think they'd just performed a miracle. Which I suppose they had, persuading so many people of all ages to leave their cosy firesides to stand around in the cold on a dark winter's night, for little more than a hot sugary drink in a polystyrene cup and a string of light bulbs.

Billy was enjoying himself now, especially after Donald had pressed more mulled wine upon him. I didn't think Joshua would have bounced back so easily.

36 Booked Up

"Thank you very much, Hector," said Dinah, slapping him hard on the back. "You've made it look so easy, I don't know why you've never published anything yourself."

Hector put the second of the two boxes of the Writers' books on the counter.

"Always the bridesmaid, never the bride, that's me."

Jessica wagged a finger at him. "Never say never."

He passed me the scissors to open the boxes.

"You're always welcome to join the Wendlebury Writers, if you'd like to," said Julia. "We're very encouraging."

Dinah gave a rare smile. "You could be our token man."

Jessica stepped in to move the conversation to safer ground.

"You don't seem very excited about the book, Sophie."

I'd been wary of speaking until now, for fear of giving away Hector's secret.

"Sorry, Jessica. Of course I'm excited. It's just – it's just that – I'd already seen the proof copy a few days ago, so I got the initial excitement out of my system then."

I opened one of the slim holly-red books at the contents page and cast my eye down the list of items.

"And it's exciting to see my name – all our names – in print. Look, we're published authors now!"

The other Writers each took a copy, turning the pages eagerly to see their own contributions, before remembering their manners and admiring the rest of the entries. They were all so engrossed with the inside of the book that it was a few minutes before they spotted Hermione Minty's endorsement on the back cover.

"Oh my word, she liked it!" Jessica squealed. "Look, Hermione Minty has actually read and enjoyed my work!"

"Our work," Dinah corrected her sternly. She read aloud what they all believed Hermione had written: "'The literary equivalent of a box of Christmas crackers, each containing a surprise, and the content carefully curated to offer something to suit every taste.'"

She looked up.

"Are you sure that's not damning with faint praise? 'Something to suit every taste' indeed. Supposing the reader's got bad taste?"

"Oh, for goodness' sake, Dinah, don't look a gift horse – don't be so ungrateful," said Bella. "I think it's completely marvellous of Miss Minty to have taken the time to read it and respond, and at such short notice too."

"She sent us a box of signed books for sale too," I said proudly, "although Hector says he won't put them out in the shop until tomorrow, so as not to distract people from our book today."

"I still think we should have asked her to come and launch it for us," said Dinah. "Don't you think so, Sophie? I mean, if you managed to persuade her to do this, maybe she'd have said yes if you'd asked her?"

I thought fast. "Her agent said she's out of the country till after Christmas."

I glanced across to Hector, calmly arranging copies of our book on the central display table.

"If she was here today, you might have found yourselves eclipsed," he said, straight-faced. "Better not to have that distraction."

I put my hand over my mouth to cover my smile. I was glad Hector was having fun. The Writers just nodded.

"Good thinking, Hector," said Dinah, whom I'd never suspected of being a Minty fan. "Why didn't you tell us that, Sophie?"

"It's just as well, considering we've got 100 copies to shift in a village of less than 1,000," said Jacky. Running her own dental practice, she had the soundest business brain of us all. "We could do without the competition."

"Oh well, perhaps we can keep her up our sleeve for another project," said Dinah. "Perhaps she'd like to join us for our reading event in the spring. A visit from her would be good for the village and the bookshop, as well as for the Writers. Public appearances are bread and butter for proper authors, you know."

"Yes, but only if you pay them," said Hector. "And I hear that to persuade Hermione Minty to appear here would require a very hefty fee indeed. Take it from me. I know these things."

"Better than any of us," I said, winking at Hector with my back to the others. I was glad his quick thinking had got Hermione off the hook. She trod a dangerous path these days.

Karen, as the only one of the Writers to have sold stories commercially, had the best appreciation of the time and effort that it had cost Hector to publish our book. She was keen to thank him in an appropriate manner. Turning her back to him, she said in a low voice to the rest of us, "I know, let's all sign our pieces in one copy and present it to Hector as a thank you gift."

"It could be worth a fortune if we all end up as famous authors," said Jessica, ever the optimist.

We huddled around to do just that, then Dinah hid the signed copy in her handbag to present to him later. After we'd rearranged the furniture in the tearoom to create a space for our readings, we took turns in standing at the lectern (a music stand borrowed from the school) to read our pieces in the book. It wasn't exactly a sound check – the shop was too small to justify using a sound system – but rehearsing gave us more confidence.

I took my turn first to free me up to help Hector prepare for opening. Then I scurried over to where he was now replenishing the children's shelves from the stockroom. He seemed introspective, and I tried to make conversation.

"They're all really pleased with the book, Hector, thank you so much." He nodded acknowledgment. "I just hope someone comes to buy them," I added, hoping for reassurance from an expert in bookselling.

I wished I'd given out more invitations the night before at the lighting up ceremony. I'd still had some left in my pocket when I got back to Hector's afterwards, and had dashed back up to the pub to leave them on the bar as a last resort. If hardly anyone turned up, I felt it would be my fault.

37 Reading Allowed

But I needn't have worried. Even before Hector had turned the sign on the shop door to "open", customers were lining up outside. I knew most of them, but there was a fair smattering of strangers. I wondered whether the lonely mother and baby would come. I wished I'd given her an invitation before she disappeared. I was feeling guilty for suspecting her as well as Carol of sabotage now. I wanted to be kind to her to make up for it.

The tearoom chairs were soon filled with an eager audience, and once all the chairs were taken, people were happy to stand at the back of the room or to sit on the floor.

"Who are all these people?" I whispered as I huddled with the rest of the Writers in the stockroom, waiting for a cue from Hector to start our performance. "There's quite a few I don't recognise."

I held the door ajar to keep watch on the arrivals.

"A few of them are my patients from the dental surgery," said Jacky. "I've had a poster up in the waiting room about it, but I didn't really expect any of them to come."

"Those young people are from my school," said Julia. "It's funny, I'm never usually nervous in the classroom, but it feels quite different to be sharing my personal writing with them, rather than plain historical facts. I'm touched that they came, and relieved that they're my better students, not the ones who graffiti rude things about teachers in the school toilets."

Finally, Hector tapped on the stockroom door, our signal to go through to the tearoom, where he said a few kind words about our book before handing over to Dinah. With commendable grace, she thanked Hector for his support and encouragement.

The readings went very well. A few members of the audience bought copies before they sat down, and Mrs Murray followed our words line by line, as if the book were a church service sheet.

When we reached the end of the final piece, Dinah, as chair of the Writers, thanked Hector for his support, then the audience for buying copies (a not-so-subtle hint to those who hadn't yet done so), and encouraged them, as I'd instructed her, to stay for some Christmas shopping and afternoon tea. Hector gave me a thumbs-up from behind the counter as the audience dispersed, most of them making at least a cursory show of browsing for other books. The rest of the Writers pushed two tables together and gathered chairs around to treat themselves to a cup of well-earned tea. I hastened behind the tearoom counter to resume my normal duties.

It wasn't until I was starting to clear the tearoom tables towards four o'clock that I noticed Damian sitting in the far corner. I hadn't served him any tea or cake, so the cheapskate must have sneaked in at the end when I wasn't looking. As I went over to remove the previous occupants' cups from his table, he pulled out a copy of the Wendlebury Writers' book from his pocket and looked up at me with a wry grin.

"Congratulations, Sophie."

That was a phrase I'd never heard from him before. I thought he'd twist it into an insult saying that I was only a big fish in a small pond. He'd have been right.

I hesitated, my cleaning cloth poised over the table. I didn't want to get his book wet. "You like it, then?"

"Yes, I think it's a real achievement. Well done."

I struggled for an appropriate reply.

"I'm touched that you bought a copy, after what you thought of my play script. And I know you like to travel light. It means a lot to me that you've found space in your van for it."

"Oh, it's not for me." He laughed. He actually laughed. "I'm going to give it to Carol for Christmas."

I bit back my disappointment. "Yes," I said quietly. "I'm sure Carol will treasure it more than you would."

Unperturbed, he scraped back his chair and stood up.

"Which reminds me, I've got to go. I promised Carol I'd water the Christmas tree on my way back."

"The one on the village green? The big one?"

"Yes, I do it about this time every night. She leaves a watering can outside the shop so I can fill it from the tap in the wall."

"And did you do it last night too, about this time?"

He gave me a disparaging look.

"What are you, my mother? It's bad enough Carol reminding me."

"And were you careful to avoid the electric box when you did so?"

He shrugged. "What electric box? I tipped it all round the base. It's always pitch dark, so I just aim at the tree. What else am I meant to do? Don't tell me there's a village tree watering technique that has passed me by. Oh, I know, a special wellspring of festive water that only bursts forth during Advent. Bloody typical."

Hector, who had been chatting outside the shop to a passer-by since going out to bring in our promotional A-board, had missed this little outburst. In blithe mood, he returned carrying the folded sign, set it down behind the door, and returned to the counter, where only a couple of dozen of our books remained.

"Good Lord, Sophie, you've very nearly sold out. Well done. Let's leave the rest of them by the till, and I'm sure they'll all go by Christmas."

I abandoned Damian and went over to join him. "Thanks for everything, Hector. We couldn't have done it without you."

He switched off the music player.

"I know. But you know the Writers couldn't have done it without you either."

"Oh, for God's sake, just listen to yourselves," said Damian bitterly, stalking out of the shop without even saying goodbye.

38 Girls on Film

"I've very nearly run out of disk space."

Having come straight to the shop from school the Monday after the dress rehearsal, Tommy pressed the play button on his camera to show me the footage. It was exciting to see the cast in costume. Suddenly the whole play started to feel real.

"If you want to keep all of this, I'm going to have to download it somewhere, so that I've got enough space to record the performance."

"That's OK, Tommy," I said. "I'm sure Hector won't mind if you dump it on to the shop's computer drive."

"Oh, won't he?" said Hector, emerging from the stockroom with a heavy box of books. "Let's watch it first, then we can decide whether it's worth keeping. I've just got to drop these text books up to the school office. You can show me the film when I get back."

I held the shop door open for him, then went to join Tommy in the tearoom, where he sat bent over the small screen.

This time, it seemed the rehearsal had gone so well that Tommy had got bored. I suppose it was hardly surprising when he'd seen the play so often that he knew most of the lines off by heart. Now he was trying to liven the proceedings up for himself by providing a running commentary.

"Oh God, what does she think she looks like?" he muttered, as the Angel Gabriel assumed a dramatic pose.

"He's much too old to be a baby's dad," was his verdict on Joseph, as Ian lifted the Baby Annabell doll from the manger to show to the shepherds.

Half way through the wise men's journey, Tommy wandered down the aisle and out of the church to stand on the gravel path, panning along the High Street. I'm not sure what he was expecting to see there – three parked camels, perhaps.

What he found on the road by the lych gate surprised us both: the side door of Damian's van sliding open, and a young woman stepping down, cradling a baby in her arms. The camera angle didn't allow us to see the face beneath her raised hood, and I couldn't be sure in the daylight, but I was almost certain that she was the mother who had stood at the edge of the crowd at the lights ceremony, before disappearing at the moment of the explosion.

Any chance of further inspection was thwarted by Tommy cutting away to the bus stop across the street. He zoomed in on a pair of teenagers canoodling in a corner of the bus shelter.

"Hold on, Tommy – can you rewind a bit please?" I asked.

"What, just when we're getting to the good bit? Don't waste the battery, it's nearly flat."

Despite the red low-power warning flashing in the corner of the screen, I reached across to press the back arrow. Damian's mysterious passenger descended from the van once more.

"Who's that girl, Tommy? Do you know her? Is she from the village?" I assumed he'd know more villagers than I did, having lived here all his life.

"I dunno. Damian's girlfriend?"

I frowned. "Damian told me he didn't have a girlfriend the day he arrived. Even if he had brought one with him, surely he wouldn't have left her in the van while he's lodging at Carol's? What sort of girl would put up with that treatment? Especially one with a baby."

Tommy shrugged. "Maybe he has to keep her locked up to stop her escaping. Maybe he doesn't want a noisy baby in Carol's house with him. Or maybe he doesn't know she's there."

"Don't be daft, Tommy. Even Damian couldn't fail to notice two stowaways in a van that size. And whose baby is it anyway?"

Tommy looked at me as if I was stupid. "Hers, of course. Unless she's some kind of travelling babysitter."

"No, no, I mean who's its father? If it's Damian's—"

I cut myself short, remembering I was speaking to a child. Too much information. And in any case, it was too humiliating to say aloud the fact that if Damian was the baby's father, he must have been two-timing me before we split up. How could I have been so naïve?

I pressed the freeze-frame button and peered more closely at the baby's face, to check for any resemblance to Damian. That wasn't easy in one so young or so blurry. Then to my annoyance, the camera screen went blank.

"I told you so, you've worn the battery out," said Tommy bitterly. "And I didn't bring the charger lead with me."

But I'd seen enough. As I leaned back in my chair, I closed my eyes, picturing the baby's thick blond hair. A baby Viking. I paid no attention to the shop door creaking open. Any customers would have to wait.

"Tommy, do you know what? I am certain the baby must be Damian's."

That was all I could bear to admit.

A gust of cold air made me turn towards the open door. Hector, just returned from the village school, was standing in the threshold, stony faced. Then he turned on his heel and marched off round the side of the shop. A moment later, I heard him start the engine of his Land Rover and drive off.

39 Father, Dear Father

"What's wrong with him?" asked Tommy petulantly, stuffing the camera back into his parka pocket. He hadn't forgiven me for wasting the last of his camera battery.

"I really don't know. But I need a cup of tea."

While waiting for the kettle to come to the boil, I made Tommy a chocolate milkshake with trembling hands. Then a text alert pinged on my phone, and I pulled it from my pocket to read it.

"I need time to think. Please lock up at closing time."

No signature. No love. No kisses. I was bewildered.

"What's up?" asked Tommy, peering across the tearoom counter to inspect my phone screen. I turned it away from him. I wanted to protect Tommy from any more bad relationship role models. He got enough of that at home.

I waited till he'd slurped up his milkshake and left the shop before deciding what to do. To my annoyance, a series of customers trickled in and out for the next half hour, and I served them as best I could, although my head was spinning. I dropped one person's change all over the floor, and when another paid by card, I hit the buttons in the wrong order three times, issuing a series of void receipts with growing embarrassment at my ineptitude.

Only when all the customers had gone, and I was setting the security alarm, did the pieces fit together. I

185

didn't know whether to be sad, hurt, offended or outraged at Hector's assumption.

Wary of conversation for fear of making things worse, I composed a careful text to set him straight. Only after hitting "send" did it occur to me that his mother or father might see it – or whoever else he had fled to. Then I locked the front door and went home.

I'd barely had time to light the woodburner before there was a knock on the door. On the doorstep stood Hector with a bunch of service station flowers in his arms, so he must have got at least as far as the motorway before he got my text.

"I feel so stupid," he said glumly.

I'd planned not to rush to forgive him, but he looked so wretched that I took his hand, rather than the flowers, and pulled him across the threshold into my arms. The bouquet fell to the floor.

"Whatever made you think it was my baby we were talking about?" I said gently into his hair. "How could I possibly be pregnant? Not with Damian's baby, anyway."

Hector pulled back and covered his face with his hands.

"I don't know. I wasn't thinking straight. It's just that it seemed as if Damian had been trying to reclaim you, and I thought—"

"Well, don't think. Please. How could it have been Damian's when I hadn't seen him since June? Did you think he'd been hiding somewhere nearby for secret liaisons with me in the meantime? Honestly, Hector! You're usually so sensible, too."

Hector dropped his hands from his face and reached out for mine.

"I'm sorry, Sophie. It was like – like a flashback to Celeste, when she deserted me for someone else, just when I least expected it. I suppose I just panicked."

I bent to rescue the bouquet, which had landed, flowers down, on the rug.

"And even if I was pregnant, do you think I'd be asking Tommy's advice about fathers? How tactless do you think I am?"

Hector slouched over to the sofa, but brightened as the news sunk in that Tommy and I had been talking about someone else.

"So whose baby has Damian fathered? Please God, don't tell me Carol's expecting."

I laughed a little sadly. "No, Carol's already told me that ship has sailed." I laid the flowers gently on my desk, and went down to sit close beside him. "I really don't know whose baby Tommy captured on film, nor who its mother or father is."

I was about to fill him in on the mysterious figure in the van, but then Hector put his arms about me, and all conversation petered out.

40 On with the Show

"You're not getting cold feet, are you, Sophie?" Hector and I stood at the back of the empty church, surveying the manger scene in the nave. In less than half an hour, at six o'clock, the church doors were due to open to admit the public.

"No, I've got my thermal socks on."

"Not that sort of cold feet, silly. I mean, about seeing your play performed in public."

I sighed. I didn't know really.

"I'm sure it'll be fine," he said briskly. "The costumes look terrific, for a start. I'm sure the audience will make allowances for the preponderance of cats and dogs."

I wrinkled my nose. "I'm not so sure about the tiger, the polar bear and the penguin, though."

"Don't worry, they'll blend in. Even the unicorn. Ian's done a marvellous job with the set."

It was true, Ian had surpassed himself. He'd persuaded John, the school caretaker, to wrestle a wooden garden gazebo from the playground into the church, and somehow they'd managed to thatch it. In a farming village, there's never any shortage of hay.

"I know. But aren't you familiar with the theatrical superstition that if the dress rehearsal goes well, the first night will be a disaster? Well, the dress rehearsal couldn't have gone better. No-one forgot a single line. And our

189

first night is our only night. We have now or never to get it right."

Hector put his arm around me, and I leaned into him for comfort. "I think you're just tired, Sophie. It's not as if it's Broadway. The New York Broadway, I mean, not the Cotswolds one."

I laughed. "But it's important to me. The cast have worked so hard at rehearsals, and all their friends and family will be coming along to support us. They mean much more to me than an audience of hundreds of strangers in a proper theatre. I don't want to let anyone down."

Or to humiliate myself in front of Damian, but I didn't say that to Hector.

"It's not as if you've had to make it up from scratch. You've just rearranged the traditional story. That strategy never did Shakespeare any harm."

"Yes, but Shakespeare I ain't."

I thought that would make my point clear.

"You're on to a winner, no matter what. No-one can complain that the plot is flawed, or that they can't work out which character is which, or what their motivation is. Your audience will be determined to enjoy it, come what may. They'll mostly be related to someone in the cast, so they'll be willing the production to succeed. You don't have to worry about technical hitches, because you're not using any technology – no lights, no microphones, no recordings. What could possibly go wrong?"

I watched Billy making a circuit of the church with a flaming taper, lighting candles on the windowsills and in various alcoves.

"Supposing the stable catches fire? Or the sheep? I bet most of those onesies are made of nylon, so they'll be inflammable."

Hector sighed.

"Don't go to meet trouble half way."

"That's what Joshua always says."

"Well, he's right. Now, have a medicinal glass of mint tea."

He led us to the trestle tables at the back of the church, and helped us to two small glasses from the samovar, one of the few souvenirs from his parents' antique shop. He'd filled it with mint tea, to go with the Middle-Eastern-themed buffet organised by the WI. The spread looked enticing, with stuffed pitta bread, samosas, bread sticks, mince pies and fingers of Christmas cake supplied by Carol's new baker, and mini kebabs and hummus with vegetable sticks from the PTA. A vast cauldron of mulled wine had been donated by The Bluebird. I hoped such a sumptuous spread would soften the audience's post-mortem on the play.

As the cooling herbal perfume began to clear my head, Carol came scuttling down the aisle towards us, blowing her taper out. She licked her fingers and pinched the tip to stop it smoking, then stuffed it in her apron pocket, already bulging with string, scissors, and bunches of safety pins. Two needles, one with white and the other with black sewing thread, were stuck through the bib of the apron, at the ready for last-minute costume repairs.

"I suggest you avoid the Christmas cake – and the mince pies may look good, but they're solid as a doorstop," she said cheerfully. "I'm going to have to cancel my trial order of that new baker chap's cakes. I've had complaints from the few customers who have bought any. But I haven't got the heart to do it till after Christmas, especially when he's given us all this tasty pizza bread and pagodas for free. Oh well, maybe the robins in the churchyard will tuck into it later. All that dried fruit will be a good source of energy in this cold weather. Do you think we'll have enough chairs?"

Hector raised his eyebrows. "I hope you've prepared a sign saying 'Standing Room Only'? Shall I go and fetch the A-board from the shop?"

I punched his arm for teasing me.

"Do you think that many people will come?"

"Oh, you'd be surprised," he said calmly. "Plenty of people come to church at Christmas who avoid it the rest of the year. Like me, for example: Exhibit A. You might think you know everyone in the village, but you meet all sorts at the Christmas services that you never see at any other time."

"Yes, they all come crawling out of the woodworms," said Carol.

"At least it proves they're still alive from one year to the next," said Ian cheerfully, emerging from the vestry in costume. His matter-of-fact approach to life and death was surprising in a village lollipop man.

"The more, the merrier," said Carol, pink with excitement. "Nice for Mr and Mrs Murray, too. Now, please excuse me. I'd better go and check everyone's all right with their costumes."

We watched her almost skip down to the vestry and disappear through the door.

"Blimey, she's a bit over-excited, even by her standards," said Ian, cheerily. "Especially considering she doesn't like Christmas."

"I suppose it must be fun for her to see her costumes put to good use after all her hard work."

I reached up to straighten Ian's headdress.

"She's been here all day on her own laying out the costumes, so maybe she's missed lunch and is getting lightheaded. I'll make her eat something before the show."

Ian tugged at the lapels of his heavy striped robe to make sure it was hanging evenly. I'd never seen him look so smart.

"The role you were born to play," said Hector, gallantly, and Ian grinned.

Then Mary, dressed as Mary, came to join us. "I hope you're not nervous, Sophie." Mary had been a constant source of reassurance to me ever since I first met her back in the summer. "It'll go like clockwork, you'll see."

I turned to check the time on the ancient clock above the vestry door. It was stuck at a quarter past two.

41 Like Clockwork

Carol was right. The church was packed. So many bodies provided a welcome warmth to the normally chilly building. Lit only by candles from altar to entrance, the whole church glowed with soft, flattering light, a detail cleverly dreamed up by Damian to create the feeling that we had gone back in time to ancient days.

Hector had tipped me off that the old box pews at the front of the church acted like human storage radiators, and he saved us seats in one. Other villagers made a beeline for the pews rather than the more comfortable chairs at the back. Just before the play was due to start, Hector and I took our seats, and were joined by the vicar's wife.

At 6pm precisely, Mr Murray processed down the aisle, followed by the church choir, resplendent in red surplices overlaid with white ruff-necked smocks. Their gold medallions glinted in the candlelight.

As the vicar climbed the spiral wooden staircase to the carved oak pulpit, the choir took their usual places in the choir stalls, ready to bolster the children's singing at strategic moments.

Mr Murray welcomed the audience and provided a brief introduction to the play, praising it as a unique coming together of so many organisations within the village. I felt very proud and not a little astonished to have been the catalyst.

When Hector squeezed my hand encouragingly, I gripped his hand with both of mine to calm my nerves.

The vicar remained in the pulpit, as if it were the Royal Box at the theatre. The cardboard hymn numbers on the board hanging beside him, ready for the Sunday service the next day, caught my eye. It was like a scoreboard. The numbers were worryingly low.

The vestry door creaked open to admit Mary, who took her place in front of the bookshelf of hymnbooks, dusting and humming to herself contentedly. The Angel Gabriel made everyone gasp by materialising from behind the curtain at the west door, where Mrs Broom had patiently hidden since before the audience arrived. Mary threw down her duster in wonder, and fell to her knees with an audible creak.

Having to turn around in my seat to watch the Annunciation scene gave me ample chance to check out the audience behind me. To my relief, all the mostly familiar faces were smiling. All except one shadowy figure, bent over on the chair nearest the door, a large shawl covering its head and shoulders. I wondered whether the person was scared of angels, and what the technical term would be for such a phobia.

My attention was distracted by the Angel Gabriel raising her arms as she began to speak, revealing glistening feathery wings that Carol had cleverly built into the bat-winged robe. She'd sewn on hundreds of creamy feathers, sequins and pearlescent beads, now twinkling in the candlelight. The audience gasped in astonishment.

Her speech over, the Angel Gabriel wafted back behind the heavy red velvet curtain that acted as a draught excluder to the side door, leaving Mary alone to digest her startling news. The audience weren't to know that while the scene unfolded, the Angel Gabriel was sneaking noiselessly out of the door and sprinting round the outside of the church, to gain readmission into the chancel via a small door beyond the choir stalls. There she was to hide until it was time for her to appear above the stable in Bethlehem.

Meanwhile, Mary was filling Joseph in on her eventful morning. He laid down his carpenter's tool bag and gave her a congratulatory hug, before pulling a scroll out of his pocket to show her the map of the journey to Bethlehem that lay ahead.

"Don't worry, I've taken care of the transport, and I got it at a bargain price, too," he told her. "We're going to need to tighten our belts if we're to have a baby."

Mary looked down at her waistline, and pulled off her generous apron to make it apparent that underneath its flowing folds she had been concealing a large baby bump.

There was a loud knock at the porch door, and a muffled clip-clop of hooves. The heavy door swung open as Tommy, dressed in a sacking tunic, proudly led in Janet the donkey, and handed her reins to Joseph. I'd been touched that Damian had thought to find a walk-on part for Tommy, until Mary had told me it was her idea.

When Tommy turned to leave, the audience chuckled at the slogan Uber Donkey Service written in Sharpie on the back of his t-shirt. Tommy turned to grin at the audience, pointing to his back in case anyone had missed the joke.

Joseph steadied Janet with her reins, and helped Mary mount the donkey side-saddle, before leading them up the side aisle and down the central one to suggest a long journey. On completion of their circuit, he stopped by the font and rapped hard on its wooden lid.

Ella Berry emerged from behind the font in her innkeeper costume.

"Good evening, sir, madam, and how can I help you?"

Ella wasn't exactly acting, just being her usual upbeat self.

"I'd like a room for the night, please, for my wife and I," replied Joseph. "This is the first time we've managed to take a mini-break from my carpenter's business, so I'd like to make this a night to remember."

A low chuckle rippled around the church.

"Hmm, I'm sorry, I'm afraid I don't have any double rooms left at all. Now, if you were younger and unattached, say, aged four to eleven, I would go out of my way to squeeze you in. New children are always welcome here."

Joseph pointed to Mary's padded stomach, now prominent beneath her flowing blue robe. "Well, I can't promise you a four-to-eleven-year-old yet, but if you give us a little time, I think you'll find our child would be a real asset to any school."

Ella stepped back in amazement, giving a stagey gasp and staring wide-eyed at Mary's bulging tummy. Her performance would have been a credit to any silent movie actress whose career had been ended by the invention of the talkies.

"Oh, my goodness, why didn't you say?" She ran a finger down the list on her clipboard. "Although our hotel rooms are all occupied, with a little extra work we could probably improvise accommodation for you, if you don't mind waiting a few moments."

She turned to call over her shoulder to summon John, the school caretaker. He emerged from the vestry carrying his school mop and bucket, his familiar brown dustcoat over a long white robe.

"John, please will you spare a few moments to do a little extra job for this nice young couple?"

Joseph patted his steely grey fringe, visible beneath his headdress, with a grin that made the congregation laugh.

"Can you just check the stable is clean and tidy? Strew some fresh straw, and—" she paused for a surreptitious look at Mary's stomach "—leave plenty of hot water, clean towels and blankets." She turned back to Mary and Joseph. "It may not be much to write home about, and you'd no doubt have a more peaceful night if you were in the inn itself, but it's certainly a room with a view. On this lovely starry night, who knows what you might see?"

42 Room at the Gazebo

The innkeeper patted the rump of Janet, the donkey, before melting away into the darkness to hide behind the font for the rest of the play.

Janet, still carrying Mary, began to advance down the nave towards the stable, with Joseph leading her by the reins. An angelic choir of schoolchildren in tinsel haloes and white tunics (plain pillowcases with strategically cut holes) processed up the central aisle. They were singing "Little Donkey" very softly. When they arranged themselves cross-legged along the chancel steps, their little bottoms must have been very cold on the ancient flagstones. They did well not to allow their song to become shriller.

Meanwhile, John had crept up the side aisle, and was waiting to welcome the party with an enamel water jug of water and a pile of fluffy towels and blankets.

Joseph helped Mary down from the donkey, then handed the reins to John, who led Janet away to a waiting mound of hay and a bucket of water in a side chapel.

Putting one hand to her aching back, Mary settled herself awkwardly on a wooden milking stool. In front of her stood a deep pine feeding trough, lined with straw and covered with a small rough blanket. Only the cast were meant to know that beneath the blanket a life-sized baby doll was waiting its cue to be born.

Joseph took down a storm lantern suspended from the roof of the gazebo, opened its glass door, lit the candle inside, and replaced the lantern on its hook. The low light glimmered romantically over the scene. I tried not to think of what might happen if the lantern fell from its nail into the manger below.

As the children finished the last verse, the Angel Gabriel arose from her hiding place and climbed up on to a concealed plinth behind the gazebo. One of the children stood up to attend to her. He picked up a bamboo cane which had been concealed behind the stable. At the top of the cane was a glowing halo, fashioned out of light sticks left over from Halloween. He positioned it neatly behind the headmistress's head and held it there.

The Angel Gabriel stood, arms raised, halo glowing, framed by the stone arches of the east window, its dark stained glass shimmering in the candlelight. Silently, the cast froze in position for a few moments, creating a dramatic tableau that might have come straight out of a medieval painting. Well, apart from the cross-legged angels, anyway.

The audience sat spellbound, waiting for the Angel Gabriel to speak.

"And lo, it came to pass that the innkeeper had been to business school and knew how to turn a crisis into an opportunity, which was just as well for Mary and Joseph. They were exhausted from their long journey. The roads were full of donkey-jams on this busiest night of the year. They appreciated the innkeeper's kindness, and Joseph decided he'd put in a good word for the hotel on TripAdvisor afterwards. They were soon comfortably settled in to their accommodation, but Mary had a funny feeling that it wouldn't be a restful night."

When the Angel Gabriel lowered her wings and put her hands together in prayer, the little angels did the same. The church fell silent again to allow the audience to absorb the peace and promise of the scene.

Then Mary stood up from her stool and stretched wearily. "I love sleeping on straw," she said. "It always smells so refreshing, and it's comfy too, provided your donkey doesn't eat it."

"Yes, the only mattress better than straw is one stuffed with feathers," said Joseph. The Angel Gabriel, raising her arms to show off her feathers, gave a look of mock horror, which made the audience chuckle.

When the laughter subsided, Joseph continued. "I'm only a humble carpenter. I'm afraid I'll never be able to afford a feather mattress for you, Mary."

The Angel Gabriel wiped her brow in relief and lowered her wings, then returned to her prayerful pose.

"I don't mind," replied Mary. "You've given me everything I need. I've really appreciated your moral support at what could have proved a very difficult time for me."

She settled herself awkwardly down on a stool, then put one hand on her cushioned tummy.

"Oh, my goodness! I think we've timed our arrival just right. How lucky are we?"

Right on cue, the organist started up an overture for the song from Handel's Messiah, "Unto Us a Son is Born", which was to be performed by the church choir. Hector had been playing Handel's Messiah a lot in the bookshop lately, and I was pleased to realise I knew all the words.

"'And His name shall be called: Wonderful! Counsellor! Almighty God! The Everlasting Father, the Prince of Peace'."

As the choir sang, the small angels got up from the steps and went to stand in a semicircle in front of the stable scene, facing the audience. Raising their arms to form a living screen, they shielded Mary's modesty during her labour. More than one of them couldn't resist waving to their families in the audience.

As the reverberations of the organ music died away, the angels slowly parted to reveal Mary, looking remarkably thinner and more composed, sitting on her stool, on top of the cushion that had provided her bump, drinking a cup of tea.

As the small angels shuffled off back to the steps, one of them turned to his friend and said loudly, "If I'd have been her, I'd have called him Joey after his dad." That wasn't in my script. I glanced up at the vicar, hoping he wasn't offended, and was relieved to see he was smiling indulgently as a ripple of laughter ran round the congregation.

I leaned across to whisper in Hector's ear.

"So far, so good."

He nodded, beaming, and squeezed my hand encouragingly.

43 Unexpected Guests

"Well," Mary was saying, "that was easier than I'd expected."

Joseph bent over the manger to tuck the blanket in around the new-born baby doll.

"Well done, dear," he said, admiringly. "Now we'd better try to get some rest."

Mary looked up and pointed down the nave.

"I don't think there's much chance of that," she said. "It looks as if we've got company."

Striding up the central aisle came one of the youngest children in a star costume, which Carol had adapted from a starfish outfit from a school production of The Little Mermaid. Behind him followed the three Wise Men, played by the school's teaching staff. Each bore an impressive gift, fashioned out of papier-mâché by the top class as their December art project.

Holding their gifts aloft for everyone to see, the trio froze into a tableau half way up the aisle, while the children gave an enthusiastic rendition of "We Three Kings". The Wise Men's arms must have been aching by the end of the last verse.

The kings resumed their journey, and when they arrived outside the gazebo, the star turned around to face them.

"Here you are, Wise Men." Then the star addressed Mary and Joseph. "Hello, I've got three Wise Men come to see you."

Mary smiled at the star encouragingly, then looked down at her baby. "Well, that's nice, dear. It's never too early to start a child's education."

The star returned to the wise men.

"Thank you, Twinkle," said the one with the gold. He reached into the pocket of his heavy emerald brocade robe, fashioned by Carol from a curtain left over from the Players' Sound of Music outfits, and fished out a nylon net bag of gold chocolate coins. Taking this gratuity, the star skipped happily up the chancel to stand on a sturdy wooden box behind the gazebo, and so appeared to come to rest over the stable.

The Wise Men approached the manger and knelt before the baby, showing a handsome profile of their headdresses to the audience.

Joseph turned to Mary with a sigh.

"So much for us travelling light, dear. I think for our trip home, we might need another donkey."

The Wise Man with the gold was first to speak.

"Gracious lady, we come not to teach your child but to learn from him. We may be Wise Men, but he can teach us so much more."

A couple of the angels sniggered at their teachers' confessions of ignorance.

"We look forward to hearing his words of wisdom once he's learned to speak," said Frankincense.

"He will be the most famous teacher and the wisest man of all," said Myrrh. "So congratulations all round."

"As a carpenter, I wish I could say he's a chip off the old block," said Joseph. "But being Wise Men, you probably already know that I can't take any of the credit for his genes."

Mary leaned over to pat Joseph on the shoulder reassuringly. "Don't sell yourself short, dear. In lots of other ways, I couldn't have done this without you. I mean, you did provide the donkey that brought us here, didn't you?"

Joseph nodded and smiled bashfully. "Glad to be of any service that I can, Mary. Just say if there's any more I can do. You know I'll always be here if you and the boy need me."

"Earthly fathers have their uses too," said Gold. He turned to face the audience with a knowing look. "Simple souls though they may be, it's always good when they turn up at parents' night at school. And speaking of simple souls, here comes a whole flock of visitors for you."

Joseph put one hand above his eyes to peer down the aisle. "Crikey, I'd better call room service for more tea."

A swarm of the youngest children had spilled out of the vestry, whispering to each other excitedly, as Sally, the chief shepherd, herded her young shepherds and lambs up the central aisle.

Meanwhile, the Wise Men arranged themselves behind the holy family. The sight reminded me of a wedding photo. The Wise Men's fancy frocks would have looked good on bridesmaids.

Despite our careful rehearsals, some of the new arrivals in the stable had forgotten the drill. Instead of arranging themselves as planned on pieces of masking tape stuck to the floor with their names on, in their excitement they buzzed around the manger like wasps round a windfall apple, jostling to see who could get closest to the crib.

Then one of the youngest piped up, "Do you think your baby Jesus would like a cuddle, Mrs Virgin?"

44 Back to the Manger

In the ensuing scuffle between the two small boys vying to be the first to pick up the Baby Jesus doll, they managed to pull it apart. This unexpected plot twist had the audience on the edge of their seats, for all the wrong reasons.

When the chilling wail rang out from the back pew and ricocheted down the aisle to the front of the church, my first thought was that it came from one of the squabbling children's parents, horrified by their irreverent behaviour.

But then the screaming woman came bounding up the aisle to join the action.

"My baby! You've murdered my baby!"

When she realised it was only a doll, she delved into the manger as if expecting to find her baby in there, which of course it wasn't.

"He was there an hour ago. I put him there myself. Who's stolen my baby?"

Poor Mary stared at her, wide-eyed. Then the woman turned to face the congregation, polling the room with an accusing finger. "All right, this is a church, isn't it? So confess? Which of you has stolen my baby?"

On the long list of things I'd worried about going wrong in my nativity play, I'd never for a moment considered the appearance of a stranger claiming we'd abducted her baby.

Even this lesser charge was mystifying. The members of the congregation looked at each other, turning this way and that, as if expecting to see one of their neighbours produce the missing child from beneath a pew, the festive equivalent of a rabbit from a conjuror's hat.

The vicar was first to pull himself together. He hammered on the pulpit's lectern to call the audience to order.

"Now, now, I'm sure there's a simple explanation. My dear girl, do I gather you have mislaid a real live baby somewhere in this building?"

The woman looked up at him dumbly. Thin as a baguette and obviously distraught, she seemed strangely familiar.

"Well, if you will leave a baby unattended, you might expect it to wander off," grumbled an elderly lady seated behind me.

"Disgraceful," agreed her companion.

"Maybe Baby Jesus caught an early flight into Egypt," said Billy, laughing at his own joke.

The vicar tried again. "So you left your baby in the manger?"

The girl nodded. "Yes. Little Arthur was nice and warm beneath the blanket. I'd just fed him so he was fast asleep. He's a very sound sleeper. I thought he'd be safe in a church. He's no trouble. He's never any trouble."

"But my dear – I'm sorry, I don't know your name – whatever possessed you to do that?"

The girl shrank back, pulling her shawl protectively about herself. "Possessed? Who said I'm possessed?"

The Angel Gabriel, channelling her inner headmistress, stepped out from behind the stable to lay one wing gently around the girl's shoulders. Then she turned to Mary and Joseph.

"Please carry on with the play, while I go and help our friend here work out what's happened to her baby. I'm sure there's a simple and satisfactory explanation."

She led the stranger gently but firmly down the central aisle towards the privacy of the vestry. In her wake, Bob, our village policeman, squeezed past the others in his pew to dash after them. The resident doctor followed suit.

Joseph, apparently remembering his designation as God's handyman, stepped up to the front of the chancel.

"Now, children, let's invite the congregation to join us in 'While Shepherds Watched'."

45 Reunited

"Sophie, you look like you've just seen a ghost," said Hector in a low voice masked by the singing. He was staring at me with concern.

I certainly felt as cold as a ghost. My thoughts were spinning so much I could hardly enunciate the words, although I'd sung along to this hymn often enough in the shop over the last few weeks. Then during the second verse, I had a flash of recognition.

"Celeste," I said faintly. "No, hang on, not Celeste."

Her child would have been much older than a baby by now.

I tugged at Hector's sleeve.

"Hector, listen, I know who that woman is and why she's here. Put Carol's hair above Billy's face."

"What?" He gave me a funny look, then glanced at Billy behind us. "What do you mean?"

"Carol's older man, her unsuitable Christmas suitor," I said slowly. "It was Bertie, Billy's brother, that she ran off with, wasn't it? Dirty Bertie?"

Hector nodded. "How did you know?"

"Because I'm willing to put money on that being Carol's long-lost daughter come back to find her. Carol was gone from the village for a whole year, wasn't she? That's long enough to have had a baby in secret, and to give it away before she returned to Wendlebury."

Hector nodded again.

"And it happened long enough ago for her daughter to have reached the age that woman is now. Though I find it hard to believe that Carol would have abandoned her baby."

Hector looked grim. "It might not have been her choice. It might have been taken from her by social services, especially if she was living in a van with an unsavoury partner."

"Then when she returned to the village, she might have kept the baby a secret to avoid hurting or shaming her parents," I said.

Hector frowned. "I suppose she could have traced the baby once her parents had died, but perhaps she was worried her daughter might not want to know her after all that time. Poor Carol."

Everything was starting to fall into place. "I bet that's what Damian was doing on my computer: secretly trying to trace Carol's long-lost daughter and bring about a reunion. Carol must have confided in him about her escapade with Bertie and the resulting child. It's a refreshing change for Damian to actually listen."

Hector shook his head. "Poor Carol, having to live with her loss for so long."

As the hymn finished, one of the little angels hiccupped loudly and giggled. The ridiculous noise acted like a "start" button to get the play moving again, with just a few lines remaining till the end.

Next thing I knew, the cast was lining up across the chancel to take their bows, and Joseph beckoned to me to come forward to receive the applause. I hesitated, till he came over to grab me by the hand and pull me up to the stable.

"Don't forget Damian," said Mary. "Where's Damian?"

46 A New Player

Everybody looked this way and that, as if Damian was the festive answer to Where's Wally. Looking back at our pew, I realised that Hector had also disappeared.

Then the vicar gave a wonderful speech that hit just the right note, saying it was the funniest nativity play he'd ever seen (I think he meant that as a compliment), and also one of the most moving.

"I'm sure that's set us all up wonderfully for the rest of Advent. My wife and I couldn't have wished for a more memorable welcome back to the village. You can always count on Wendlebury Barrow to be that little bit different and inventive. The Wendlebury way, ha ha. And that very special interpretation of the story of Jesus's birth will be popping in and out of our heads all over Christmas."

The vicar blessed the congregation, then urged us to stay and enjoy the lovely spread that had been laid out at the back of the church. I returned to the pew as people filed down the aisles towards the buffet tables, gossiping and chattering no doubt about the mysterious intruder. Their children ran from the front to rejoin their families, as eagerly as lambs in a field finding their ewes.

I sat down hard on the pew, and stared for a while, glassy-eyed, at the stable, which had been the focal point of my ambitions these last few weeks. Unable to believe it was all over, I felt strangely deflated.

I don't know how long I'd sat there when I felt a warm hand clamp down on my shoulder. I recognised Damian's touch.

"Sophie," said Damian's voice. "There's someone I'd like you to meet."

"Really?" Adrenaline surged through me. I shot to my feet, recognising the sound of a baby gurgling behind me, and spun round.

There stood Damian with his arm round the girl. Carol stood beside her, flushed with excitement, cuddling a real live baby against her chest. Hector hovered behind them, his hand on Carol's shoulder.

"This is Becky," said Damian. "Carol's daughter. And her grandson, Arthur."

"I know," I said quietly. "I'd just guessed."

Unusually for him, Damian chose that moment to step out of the limelight and drift away towards the buffet.

"Hello, Sophie," said the girl, in a quiet voice. "I'm sorry for spoiling your play."

I slumped back down on to the pew.

"Oh, don't worry about that, you didn't spoil it," I said. "The play was just fine. You carry on."

Carol, murmuring gently to the baby, took him for a walk to the chancel to show him the manger scene. Becky followed close behind her, reaching a hand out as if unsure whether Carol might run off with him.

Hector lingered behind with me, watching after them.

"You were right, Sophie," he said. "Carol had taken Damian into her confidence. Of course, I knew about Carol and Bertie, as did Billy, and a few other older folk in the village. But no-one ever knew that Carol had had a baby, until she told Damian. Apparently the baby was

218

taken away from her by social services for its own safety, because of Bertie's violence. What an awful thing to happen."

Carol and Becky were talking shyly to each other. Carol had started to show Becky points of interest in the church, then slowly they became less aware of their surroundings and gazed only at each other, registering their undeniable bond.

"The likeness is uncanny when you see them together," Hector agreed. "I've seen photos of Carol at Becky's age, and they could be the same person."

"It's like watching the same person thirty years apart," I whispered.

Then Hector frowned.

"What on earth made you mention Celeste when she first appeared? Surely you didn't think it was Celeste come back to haunt me all the way from Australia?"

I thought fast. "Oh, I didn't mean your Celeste. I was just naming angels. Celeste is a popular name for an angel, isn't it, like Gabriel? Perhaps I've just been spending too much time in the company of angels lately."

47 Director's Cut

With perfect timing, Jemima and two of her little friends marched up to us with a couple of plates of Middle Eastern snacks. "The dinner ladies said we've got to give you these." They meant the WI.

The array of bite-sized pittas, falafels, dates, olives and grapes looked delicious, and I realised how hungry I was.

"Thanks, girls, and well done," I said, as we each accepted a plate gratefully. "You did brilliantly in the play."

They giggled and ran back down the aisle, whispering excitedly to each other. I bit gratefully into a date, but then nearly choked on it as I remembered the most important thing.

"But what happened to the baby? How had he got into the manger, and how did he disappear?"

Hector paused, a falafel halfway to his mouth.

"Apparently while Carol was in the church on her own, laying out the costumes before the cast arrived, she heard a snuffling in the chancel. She went to investigate, pulled back the blanket, and found a baby fast asleep. Thinking he had been abandoned, she picked him up and carried him back to the vestry to look after him while she worked out what to do next. Not wanting to disrupt the play, she hid him in the wardrobe, where the vicar's robes are stored, and she stayed in the vestry with him till the play was over to make sure he was OK. Despite all the noise, the baby didn't wake up till he heard his mother's cry of distress. Which is rather touching when you think about it."

"And remarkably obliging of the baby. Still, Becky did say he's a good sleeper. But how did he come to be in the manger in the first place, if that isn't a silly question?"

"Becky had left him there, thinking that if she presented the baby to Carol in front of the whole village, she'd be less likely to turn them away. Becky was used to being turned away by people. Arthur's father did a runner before the baby was even born."

"Poor Becky, and poor Arthur."

At that point, Damian came striding up to us cheerfully, a glass of mulled wine in one hand and a plate piled high with food in the other. I guessed the WI had fallen for his charms too.

"I bet you didn't see that plot twist coming," he grinned.

I turned on him. "Damian! What the hell did you think you were playing at, interfering in Carol's secret past?"

"If what you mean, Sophie, is was it my idea to track down Carol's long-lost daughter, then yes, it was. But only after Carol had told me about Becky, and made it clear how much she regretted having to give her up as a baby. She had no idea that Becky had a baby too. I only found out once I'd traced her and gone to meet her for the first time in my van."

I felt slightly mollified.

"But it was bloody difficult to get Becky to hook up with Carol once I'd got her down here," said Damian. "She was too nervous of rejection, too worried that Carol wouldn't want to know her. As if! So, as you may have guessed by now, she's been living in my van for the last couple of weeks, getting up the nerve to meet her long-lost mother."

"In your van? In December? Damian, how could you let her?"

He looked at me evenly. "Sophie, if I've learned anything since I came here, it's that I can't make women do what they don't want to do."

48 Exit, Pursued by a Donkey

Hector, setting down his empty plate, quietly looped his arm round me, as if staking his claim. Damian went on speaking, his mouth full of pitta bread.

"Becky told me she was going to take Arthur to the church to introduce him to Carol, while I went to fetch Janet, the donkey. She must have chickened out. By the time I got back, I had to get straight on with directing the play. I just assumed they'd hooked up and all was fine. It never occurred to me that she might have done something that mad."

Carol and Becky were now sitting in the choir stalls, playing with the baby together. He seemed an exceptionally good-natured child. To look at them, you'd think they'd known each other all their lives.

"I suppose I can understand why she'd behave that way if she was worried about rejection. I mean, who's going to reject a baby found in a manger in the run-up to Christmas? But hang on, Damian, anyone could have come along and carried the baby off. Then where would she be?"

Damian shook his head. "Oh no, Becky had planned to come forward the minute the baby was discovered, and announce herself to Carol and everyone then. She is a very good mother. She adores little Arthur."

"But, Damian, she let him sleep in your van!"

Damian put his finger against his lips to silence me. "Don't let her hear you say that. She's been in places a lot worse. Lived in a squat for a while after her boyfriend ditched her. Maybe now she's landed on her feet at last."

"Why didn't you say something sooner?"

As I had been Carol's friend long before Damian was, I felt irked to be late to the party.

"I'm sorry I couldn't tell you before, Sophie. But Becky wouldn't let me say anything to anyone until she was ready, and I respected that. It took all my dramatic powers to persuade her to come to the village at all, bigging up how sad and lonely Carol is. Although—" he looked at his feet "—I didn't need to exaggerate."

I nodded.

"I drove down to Brighton to collect her from this awful hostel she was living in, then when we got back here, she refused to come out of the van. When I told her about your nativity play, she dreamed up the mad notion that it would be the perfect time to reveal herself and her baby to Carol. What else could I have done? I could hardly throw her out of the van, could I?"

I looked up to the chancel, where Carol and Becky were standing close together by the manger, Arthur in his grandmother's arms. Carol looked as if she'd just opened the best Christmas present she'd ever had.

"No, Damian, you did the right thing. It can't have been easy for you either."

Carol looked up and saw me watching them, and beckoned us all over.

"Sophie, isn't my grandson gorgeous? He and Becky have come to spend Christmas with me."

For the first time, Becky smiled.

"And maybe a bit longer," added Carol.

Damian looked smug. "Well, there you go, Carol. You kept saying I was the son you never had, and now you've got your daughter back, and a grandson as a bonus. I was just the understudy. Now the play's over, and all's right with the world, I think my work here is done."

He stepped back, and I knew he was going to have one of his dramatic moments. He recited grandly, gesturing at the features of the church around him:

> *"'Our revels now are ended. These our actors,*
> *As I foretold you, were all spirits and*
> *Are melted into air, into thin air:*
> *And, like the baseless fabric of this vision,*
> *The cloud-capp'd towers, the gorgeous palaces,*
> *The solemn temples, the great globe itself,*
> *Yea, all which it inherit, shall dissolve*
> *And, like this insubstantial pageant faded,*
> *Leave not a rack behind. We are such stuff*
> *As dreams are made on, and our little life*
> *Is rounded with a sleep'."*

"'The Tempest'," said Becky, shyly, looking up at him from under her long lashes. "Prospero's speech."

"Bloody hell," said Damian, wide-eyed. I glanced at Hector, who was smiling approvingly.

For a split second, Carol looked disappointed. "Does that mean you're off, then, Damian?"

He nodded.

"Yes. Call me Mary Poppins. I suspect that's more up your street than Prospero, Carol. And yours, Sophie."

He winked at Becky.

"You don't need me any more. None of you do." He shot me a reproachful glance. "So I'll be off to my folks in Northampton tonight, then back to Spain with the rest of my theatre company for the New Year. I thought we might have time to squeeze in an improvised panto before our spring tour starts." He flashed his best smile. "Your script has inspired me, Sophie."

Coming from Damian, this was praise indeed. I didn't even mind that he was comparing my nativity play to a pantomime.

"So I'll be out of your hair, Carol, and Becky can have my room."

Becky looked up at him, her eyes filled with tears. She spoke in a small, quavering voice. "Damian, I don't have the words to thank you."

"No thanks required," he said briskly. "If Carol hadn't been so kind to me, it wouldn't have happened. I'm just glad I was able to return the favour she did me. You did ask for payment in kind, didn't you, Carol?"

Carol, for once, was rendered speechless. She bent her head to kiss the now sleeping baby's forehead.

"Anyway, you'll have to excuse me now. I've got a date with a donkey before I shoot off – got to return Janet to Stanley. Then my matchmaking duties will be over for the night."

Becky threw her arms around his neck, then clung to him for a moment while shedding a few tears of gratitude. Then, to my surprise, Carol pressed the baby into my arms to free herself to hug them both together.

49 A Christmas Feast

"So, time to send out for the biggest turkey in the shop?" asked Hector, mischievously once Damian had gone.

Becky turned to Carol.

"Actually, I'm vegetarian," she said anxiously. "I hope you don't mind?"

Carol laughed. "Of course not, my dear. And anyway, I don't usually have a turkey at home at Christmas. I volunteer at the homeless shelter in Slate Green on Christmas Day and eat there with the clients. You can come and help, if you like? Little Arthur would bring a smile to their faces, I'm sure."

Becky's eyes were wide. "You're one of those volunteers? That's amazing. You change lives, people like you."

I guessed she'd passed through a lot of shelters like that in her time.

Any further conversation on that score was cut short by the arrival of Tommy, who came bounding across from the buffet table carrying a plate piled high with food, eager to add his twopenn'orth. He'd turned his t-shirt back to front now, to make sure no-one missed its slogan.

"Finish your mouthful first, please, Tommy," I said, picking a damp speck of his falafel off my top.

We all waited expectantly to see what he was so eager to tell us. He swallowed hard.

"The thing is, Sina was wrong about my mum's baby," he said cheerily. "I mean, she isn't having one. But I've still got that board book I bought for it. Do you think your baby would like it, miss? I mean, I know what it's like to grow up without a dad. You don't get so many presents. I'd really like to give the board book to your baby."

I'd forgotten how fast news travelled in this village.

"Thank you, I'm sure he'd love it," said Becky, with a tremor in her voice. "Perhaps you'd like to read it to him some time."

"But it's got no words in it," said Tommy, puzzled.

"No, but you can make up a story about the pictures in it. Just sit him on your lap and show him the pictures. He'd like that."

Tommy's shy smile suggested he would too, and he sloped off back towards the buffet, looking pleased.

Next Kate came striding down the aisle to join us.

"Babies, eh, aren't they great?" she cried cheerfully, tickling Arthur under the chin with a perfectly manicured finger. "I suppose you might call this one a proper godchild since he was left in a manger. Still, children, godchildren, they're all great, aren't they? I love babies. Becky, come and look at the font with me. Perhaps you'd like to have him christened here."

"Ooh, Becky, what a lovely idea," said Carol, following Kate and Becky down the aisle.

Something else suddenly made sense to me. "Hector, how many godchildren has Kate got?"

Hector looked surprised. "Just me, I think, and my cousin James in Australia."

"And is there such a thing as a great-godchild?"

"No, not really. A child is either your godchild or they're not. It's all determined by who takes the vows at the child's christening. It doesn't pass down a line genetically like parenthood. And certainly not in Kate's case, because neither James nor I have any children. Of course, James is only six, so he'd be a bit young for it, but he's a great kid."

A great godchild, in fact. Not Celeste and Hector's child at all.

I slipped my hand into Hector's. "I think I could do with another glass of mulled wine."

50 A Change of Heart

As Hector and I stood by the font, sipping mulled wine from paper cups, watching Carol and her new-found family chatting away, Damian strolled down the aisle to collect Janet from the side chapel.

"You know, I think you might have been a bit harsh on old Damian, Sophie," said Hector.

I spluttered into my cup. I wondered whether he'd have been so magnanimous if Damian hadn't been about to leave the village.

"Aren't you going to say goodbye to him?" added Hector. "I think perhaps you should."

I gave Hector my cup to refill, then went over to catch Damian and Janet, just as they were about to head out through the porch door. Damian turned around at the sound of my footsteps on the flagstones.

"Sophie?"

I stopped a few paces short of him, aware that Hector might be watching, and not wanting to give him unnecessary cause for jealousy.

"Damian, I wanted to say thank you for all you've done. Not just for directing the play – which was brilliant, by the way – but for being so kind to Carol. What you've done, bringing Becky and Arthur to the village, will be life-changing for her and for them all. She's been so lonely since her parents died."

Damian stroked Janet's mane. "She was very kind to me too. She needn't have been. She didn't know me from Adam. Now I'm just a cuckoo in their nest."

"Yes, but at least you tarted the nest up while you were there. You did a good job, Damian. You earned your keep. But I'm so glad to hear Becky's staying. How wonderful!"

"Well, let's see how they get on long term. It's early days yet. But you know what? I've got a good feeling about this. They both need it to work."

I knew he was right, but I so wanted Carol to find a happy ending. I gazed at him in silence for a moment.

"You've changed, Damian," I said.

"I know," he said gently. "Thanks to you and Wendlebury Barrow. Still, that's what village life is all about, isn't it? Community? Family? All that slushy stuff? Now, back to reality for me. I'd better hit the road. I told my folks I'd be at theirs by bedtime, and I've got to get this donkey parked up first."

I reached out to stroke Janet's mane. She really had been no trouble at all.

"I suppose you'll be spending your Christmas with Hector, then?" Damian asked lightly.

I shook my head. "No, we're both off to our respective parents. I'm catching a plane to Inverness last thing tonight, and he'll be driving down to Clevedon on Christmas Eve after he's closed the shop for the holidays."

He looked down at Janet's gentle face for a moment, then tugged at the donkey's reins to make her walk on. She didn't move.

"Children and animals, eh? There'll be none of either in my next production. Apart from a pantomime horse, maybe."

"Thanks, Damian, for all you've done. Take care and have fun in Spain."

He raised his eyebrows suggestively. "Don't worry, I will."

Recognising the old Damian once more, I felt a sudden pang of loss. I realised I might never see him again. After all, we had history. I'd spent most of my adult life in league with him.

In the darkness of the church porch, I reached up to give him a gentle farewell kiss on the cheek. My senses jolted at the familiar brush of stiff Viking hair against my brow.

Then with a clip-clop across the flagstones, Janet followed him out into the night.

I dashed back to the font, worried that Hector might be upset if he'd seen me kiss Damian. He hadn't even noticed. Deep in conversation with the baker, he was waving a stuffed pitta bread in one hand.

"This is fabulous," he was saying. "You ought to get Carol to stock these in the shop."

I wondered whether I was the only one to notice the baker's eyes brighten at this point.

"I'm afraid we don't do savouries in my bookshop tearoom, only cakes, but if we ever diversify into lunches – make a mental note of that thought, Sophie – I'd definitely like to include some of these in the menu. What do you think, sweetheart?"

He held out his pitta for me to take a bite. I chewed thoughtfully and waited till I'd swallowed before giving my verdict. "Very good, really light and fluffy. Not like a supermarket pitta at all."

The baker was gazing across the church at Carol.

"Thanks, but I'm thinking that cakes are my best bet financially. There's more potential profit in fancy cakes, which is why I've made them the lynchpin of my new business. I have taken some samples into the village shop, but I'm not sure Carol wants to stock them in the new year."

My heart melted at his anxious look. I quickly made some excuses for her to spare his feelings. "She has been a bit preoccupied lately, getting all the costumes ready for the play. Why don't you pop back next week before Christmas to ask her?"

With his hands in his pockets resignedly, he continued to stare at Carol, now engrossed in watching the baby play with a breadstick. "Is that her daughter and grandson?" His voice wavered.

"Yes." I smiled. "I expect you can see the family likeness."

"Yes, her daughter's beautiful too," he said.

I looked at him in surprise. I'd never thought of Carol as being beautiful before, but I could see now that when she was Becky's age, she must have been. Through the baker's eyes, she was beautiful still, especially in the candlelight, pink and animated with excitement.

"Is – is her husband here?" he asked, sounding as if he feared the answer. "I thought she was single."

He turned his puppy-dog eyes on me.

"No, there's no husband, no Mr Carol." I tried not to smile. "Ooh, I don't suppose you know the time, do you?"

He pulled back his cuff to check. "Just gone half seven. Sorry, am I keeping you?"

Hector butted in. "Sophie has a flight to catch from Bristol Airport in a little while. She's off to spend Christmas in Inverness with her parents, so we really need to get going, I'm afraid."

He grabbed my arm and began to steer me towards the door.

"But do chase Carol up," I called over my shoulder. "Offer her your savouries instead of the cakes. And merry Christmas!"

I turned to Hector. "That was a bit rude, dragging me off like that."

"I thought you were trying to get away from him. He is a bit dull."

I stopped by the hymnbook table. "No, not at all. Don't you see? I was trying to detect whether he was married. He had his hands in his pockets. I'd spotted he was right-handed, so I knew that his watch would be on his left wrist. When I asked him the time, it was only to get him to expose his left hand so I could check for a wedding ring."

"He doesn't strike me as the marrying kind."

That's what Carol said about you, I thought, but didn't say it.

Now that people were starting to leave the church, the vicar had taken up his post in the porch, shaking hands with his parishioners as they passed by. As we reached the front of the queue, he took my outstretched hand in both of his and held it steady, fixing me with the big brown eyes of one of Santa's reindeer.

"Sophie, that was marvellous. You managed to inject new zest and fun into the nativity story and make it relevant and engrossing for the villagers, while also keeping alive the awe and wonder about our Lord's birth. Kate tells me you're a trained teacher. I wonder whether you'd care to help her restart the village Sunday School? I feel sure you have a special talent for interesting young minds in the teachings of the church."

His smile was so winning and his hands so warm that I found myself faltering an almost soundless, "Yes, of course." I felt as if he had cast a spell over me.

51 A Toast to Christmas

Hector and I walked down the path hand in hand towards the lychgate, our other hands warming round polystyrene cups of mulled wine. As our feet crunched on the gravel, I was already regretting how easily the vicar had won me over. I'd never meant to volunteer.

Hector found the idea of me teaching Sunday School amusing.

"Look out, Sophie. With those powers of persuasion, he'll have you taking holy orders before January is out. 'Get thee to a nunnery.'"

"I assume that's a quote rather than a command?"

"Hamlet, to Ophelia. And don't, by the way. It didn't do Ophelia any good."

I turned the conversation on a different tack. "To be honest, I haven't spared a thought for January yet. I've been so focused on getting the nativity play out of the way, I'm not ready for a new year."

"No, but I bet you're ready for a break."

I stopped still on the frosty pavement, mouth open. Surely he wasn't going to break up with me tonight of all nights?

He pulled at my hand to make me walk on. For a moment, I felt like Janet.

"And after you've had a nice break with your parents, maybe—" he coughed "—when you get back, you'd like to come down in the New Year and meet mine?"

I stopped again, stunned by the enormity of what Hector, the self-confessed commitment-phobe, had just said. I drained my mulled wine, then threw my arms round him, crushing my polystyrene cup like a melting snowball. At first I was unable to speak, but that might have been partly because I'd just swallowed a clove.

Then my voice returned.

"Yes," I said. "Yes, I will. Yes."

"But first, before I drive you to the airport, let's go back to my flat for a quick nightcap. We don't need to leave till about nine."

"But you're driving. And you've just had mulled wine. You'd better not drink any more alcohol."

Marching faster now, he squeezed my hand to reassure me, his face deadpan. "Who said anything about having a drink?"

I hastened my step.

Coming Soon

Meanwhile, the baker noted with a sigh that while his pitta wraps had quickly disappeared, most of his mince pies had remained untouched. Accidentally he knocked one on to the floor, where it landed with a thud but remained entirely intact.

He thought everyone loved mince pies at Christmas, but now these would all be wasted. He couldn't really sell them after they'd been out on display all evening.

Or could he? It wasn't as if they were sausage rolls or meat pies. They wouldn't give anyone food poisoning. Mincemeat lasted for ages, didn't it? A bit like jam. He tried to remember his recent training. Considering he'd downshifted from accountancy to a craft to reduce his stress levels, he was still having far too many anxious moments.

Still, there were perks. Like the lovely, warm-hearted Carol. When he came back from loading the empty pitta trays and boxes of uneaten mince pies in his van, he was disappointed to find she'd gone, taking her daughter and grandson with her.

After saying goodbye to the WI ladies who were still clearing away, the baker retreated to his van, where he sat for a few minutes trying to summon up the courage to call on Carol on his way home. Then he realised that he had no idea where she lived.

After cleaning his sticky hands on a wet-wipe, he reached over to extract from the glove compartment a large glittery Christmas card featuring a jolly snowman and snowlady, holding snow hands and smiling sweetly. With a deep intake of breath, he pulled a pen from his pocket, opened the card, and signed his name, quickly adding a small kiss. He stared at it, wondering whether it looked too stark. Then he added "Happy Christmas Carol" at the top and stuffed it quickly in the envelope before he could change his mind.

He was just about to seal the envelope when he realised he'd forgotten the comma between "Christmas" and "Carol", which would have made him look foolish and ignorant. A "merry Christmas carol" was not what he meant at all.

Reckless now, he added another two kisses, and licked and sealed the envelope before his courage could fail. Then he started the engine, pulled out on to the High Street, and drove towards the village shop.

As he passed Hector's House, a low light flicked on in the front room of the flat above the bookshop. He ought to call in there after Christmas, he thought, to see if that nice chap with the curly hair would place a regular order for his cakes. He was kicking himself for not suggesting it earlier, when the young couple had complimented him on his pitta bread. He wasn't much good at this marketing lark.

Pulling on the brake outside the village shop, he looked for signs of life, but all was in darkness. He got out of the car to read the opening times on the window sticker, and discovered to his relief that the shop would open every day until Christmas, closing only at noon on Christmas Eve. Carol would definitely get his card in good time.

He posted it through the letterbox, waiting to hear it fall on the doormat. The point of no return. Then he pulled himself together, got back in his van and slipped into first gear. As he made for home in Slate Green, he was full of hope as to what the New Year might bring him in the village of Wendlebury Barrow – perhaps a role as the Ghost of Carol's Christmas Yet to Come.

THE END

If you enjoy reading this book,
you might like to spread the word to other readers
by leaving a brief review online –
or just tell your friends!
Thank you.

For the latest information about Debbie's
books and events, visit her Writing Life website, where
you may also like to join
her free Readers' Club:

www.authordebbieyoung.com

Acknowledgements

Enormous thanks to all the people who have helped make this a better book:

- Alison Jack, my editor, always patient, capable, and dependable
- Lucienne Boyce, David Penny, Belinda Pollard and Orna Ross, for wise and sensitive mentoring and moral support
- Simon Bendry, for his expert advice about Remembrance Day procedures
- Shaun Ivory, a sage Irish writer friend who always keeps me on my toes and encourages me to keep striving for more
- Michael MacMahon, whose wonderful delivery of Prospero's speech to close each Hawkesbury Upton Literature Festival inspired me to include it in this story

All seven of these are also authors, and I highly recommend their books.

Rachel Lawston, of Lawston Design, has done a marvellous job of the cover, helping to bring the book and the Sophie Sayers Village Mystery series to life at a glance. Her service is creative, generous and wise, and I count myself very lucky to be her client.

Finally, many thanks to Lucinda May Somerville, who, eons ago, when we were at the University of York together, gave me for my twenty-first birthday the small blue hardback volume of the York Mystery Plays mentioned in this book, with the inscription: "Maybe it'll remind you of York when you get decrepit." I hope she'll be glad that I put it to constructive use eventually.

With very best wishes
Debbie Young

Also by Debbie Young

Sophie Sayers Village Mysteries
Best Murder in Show
Trick or Murder?
Murder by the Book (coming spring 2018)

Short Story Collections
Marry in Haste
Quick Change
Stocking Fillers

Single Short Story Ebooks
Lighting Up Time
The Owl and the Turkey
The War of the Peek Freans Light Wounded

Essay Collections
All Part of the Charm:
     A Modern Memoir of English Village Life
Young By Name:
     Whimsical Columns from the Tetbury Advertiser